BEN DIAZ is an Irish New Zealander, who lives in Cornwall. He has lived in Hong Kong, Singapore, Aden, Germany and Great Britain. He is a fine artist, photographer, poet, language teacher, art historian, public speaker and popular musician. He lives with his partner in Cornwall and he has three grown-up daughters. He is a fluent and keen Francophile, and speaks three Latino languages. He has a keen interest in sports, especially rugby and cricket, and likes deep-sea fishing in the Bahamas and big game hunting in Africa, in the grand tradition of that great hunter-writer, Ernest Hemingway.

He takes an active interest in his local community in Cornwall, and he is currently working on his latest novel, about pirates and smugglers over three generations, who serve with Sir Francis Drake in 1588 and Horatio Nelson in 1805.

MERMAID

MERMAID

Ben Diaz

ATHENA PRESS
LONDON

MERMAID
Copyright © Ben Diaz 2007

All Rights Reserved

ISBN 10-digit: 1 84401 969 1
ISBN 13-digit: 978 1 84401 969 4

First Published 2007 by
ATHENA PRESS
Queen's House, 2 Holly Road
Twickenham TW1 4EG
United Kingdom

Printed for Athena Press

Chapter One

The sun set over the bay. The mini-golf course two hundred yards inland saw just a few players driving and wedging their way through the green fairways.

The children, both aged about ten, were fighting as the water foamed upon the rocks.

And then they saw it.

'Oi, look at that Nat!'

'You mean this? It's like a beautiful queen's coronation crown.'

'If I wear it on my head I will be the queen of the Commonwealth!'

The words rippled off the tongue with the confidence of true childhood; that truth which defied grown-up logic. Words that believed the impossible to be everyday life. A child's world, without boundaries or hindrances of the bigger world which demands facts and proof. A scientist's nightmare but a child's dream.

The older of the two children grabbed the stone awkwardly and feasted her eye on the object. It was about three inches long by one inch wide and there was grime and sand ingrained on the surface. At the edge was a glint of sparkling light reflecting the afternoon sun.

'We'll keep it,' Ophelia announced grandly. 'It will serve me well in my kingdom where I am Queen of the Fairies. I will give it my healing powers for I can do anything I like in my world. You put it in your bum bag and we'll see what we can do with it. It will be my jewel of greatest value, just you see, Nat!'

Natalie and Ophelia took their leave and together, hand-in-hand, they trundled happily towards the house at the side of the bay.

The sun had just gone down and the children hurried, afraid of the anger of their nanny which could resort in a smack on their hands or their bottom. Nanny was not concerned with new principles of sparing the children. She was paid a princely sum for her services and she would turn them into women of high moral fibre with the grace that transcends class or quality.

'Come along now or I'll lose my temper,' said Nanny towering over them with mock anger. They fell into line like unruly soldiers at a dawn parade.

'Hurry up, Natalie. Come on, Ophelia,' the words rat-tatted into the evening silence, resounding through the monied building, right to the drawing room.

Klimt prints surveyed the room and a Giacometti sculpture looked down from the mantelpiece auspiciously, its uneven surface cast in bronze, highlighted its quintessential fibre. The room was decorated in good taste. There was parquet flooring in varnished red and at the centre of the flooring stood a long handsome Indian Numbdah rug, which was imperfect because it was the only item in the room that *was* perfect. It was multi-coloured with jagged edges at the centre and the sides. Adorning the room sat a Habitat-like settee with beige piping on the edge of its cushions together with North American Indian patterns. It was all superbly decorated. A Bronze ballet dancer pirouetted across the G-plan occasional table and two ashtrays, chunky and transparent, sat upon the small table in the centre of the room. Lights with five-foot high shades hung from the ceiling. It had the look of an interior designer's touch. The girls lived with their father, an influential civil servant with exquisite connections to the cabinet. This was one of his four residences and he could afford the best – old money, not the oppressive garishness of the *nouveau riche*. The house reflected its owner; a man of wealth and influence.

Yet the girls saw little of their father. They hid behind material possessions and lived in their perfect world of certainty ruled only by the ministrations of Nanny Pierce.

Nanny Pierce was a handsome woman; handsome rather than pretty. She was tall and God-like to the girls. She possessed a roman nose with sumptuous lips that smiled at you at the sides. She was muscular underneath the uniform skirt and blouse and she revelled in the masculinity of the sexually unfulfilled woman.

Despite all that, Nanny Pierce possessed a serene countenance that glistened from within. She rarely had to raise her voice. A raised eyebrow here, a stern glare there, ruled the children in a secure and loving land of just values. Nanny Pierce had loved a man who was killed in the Battle of Britain in 1940; she had since dedicated her life to sculpting impressionable young lives. In this vocation she had few equals and earned a salary that reflected her importance. The girls would never forget her.

'Have you got our prize?' Ophelia hissed. Natalie nodded. She took it out of her bum bag and showed it proudly.

'Put it on your chest of drawers so we won't forget it.' Natalie complied, the younger serving the elder as a matter of course. They were twins, but not identical twins. They had a verbal currency all of their own and often launched into it when besieged by grown-ups. They knew each other's needs instinctively. Natalie knew that Ophelia – always the neat one – would relax now that their prize was in a safe place. They smiled at each other, oblivious to the horrors of the less favoured families. Their world was centred in love. They would remain close until death, and they possessed intuition that caused them to forsake reason or argument. They ate dinner in contented silence. Nanny Pierce made polite conversation and they contributed just enough but their minds were on the stone.

Perhaps it was valuable! Could it be stolen? How come it was on the beach? The junior feelings under their breasts were seen by Nanny who could guess what they were thinking. They often became like this and Nanny assumed it to be some game they were playing. She chose not to invade their world and indulged them by staying silent.

Dinner was over.

They scampered up to their room and locked the door. This was a privilege accorded them as long as they obeyed the rules of the house. Nanny smiled benignly. She had a new book she wanted to read so everyone was happy for the evening. Mr Prendergast-Bell would ring at eight and she'd report that all was well. He'd curtly ring off. Then the evening would be hers.

Ophelia put the stone in her hand. She lay on her bed. Then she felt weaker and weaker. Was it her imagination? She felt she was going down a spiralling staircase. She stuck with the stone and the experience as it got more real. Before she went out cold she dropped her hands and the stone fell down. Slowly her faculties returned to her. Ophelia felt groggy. She told Natalie. Natalie eyed the stone as her sister spoke then she said with a firmness of forethought, 'We'll take it to our hiding place tomorrow.' Their hiding place was over the bay in the common land in the tropical island of Mulatta. It took them twenty minutes to get there at walking pace. So they slept the sleep of the just.

Their home was a tropical island favoured by the rich and famous and the girls had a tutor – a well spoken young man who grounded them in Latin, Greek and mathematics. Nanny took them in languages and spiritual oversight. Their father saw them for two weeks in the summer, one week at Christmas and on holidays from his hush-hush highly responsible and absurdly well-paid post.

The next day their minds were on their adventure.

When three o'clock came they rushed upstairs and placed the stone in Natalie's bumbag. To get to their hidey-hole the girls had to go through the poor sector of town and through the wasteland in order to reach the plateau of grassland. Oblivious to the rights and wrongs of life, Ophelia and Natalie set out together. Nanny Pierce waved them goodbye.

As they hopped, skipped and jumped along the pathway they didn't notice a large teenage boy in jeans and trainers following them.

'Come here, rich bitches!' he hissed. Ophelia and Natalie turned in fear to confront their enemy.

'My daddy will punish you if you are nasty to us,' Ophelia spoke proudly. A punishing pang jawed its way through her innards which whipped at her senses and splodged her onto the cement path. A sharp stabbing pain reached her stomach and she vomited. Without saying a thing the young man ripped the bum bag from Natalie, whose eyes never left his, like a mongoose viewing a king cobra. She felt the slap of the rubber belt whack against her hips as he pulled it from her, but she kept quiet. Ophelia always spoke for her. He opened the bag. He inspected the stone quickly, looked nonchalant and put it in his pocket. He shoved the girls away. They were only too happy to go. He watched them in the distance. He was eighteen and possessed the cockiness of adolescence which told everyone he knew everything there was to know about life. He had been the biggest at school which he'd left three years ago. He was an addict. The veins were blue in the V of his forearms. He'd turned on those rich girls in desperation.

The emotions which were repressed compared to the intellect that might have given him a way out through island cricket were to the fore. He surveyed the stone, unsure of its real value. Perhaps the old man at the corner of town who owned the pawn shop would give him a tenner for it. He didn't know. He cussed, jerking inside, his body insistent for its kiss of death. He was touchy when he needed gear. And he was dangerous. The stone looked good and it was heavy. The gleaming spot inside it told him it was worth something. He hurried to the other side of town with a sense of urgency. His body screamed from within. If he hadn't needed a fix so much he'd have ravaged those girls. The bigger one's knickers flashed through his senses even now. He'd get them next time. They thought the world belonged to them. He cussed inwardly at the cruelty of birth and moved python-like through the afternoon neighbourhood. He needed that fix. He hadn't time to show it to Charlie, his boss. He had to get to the old man and get a tenner for a hit of heroin. His life depended on it.

The old man looked impassively into Karl's eyes. His eyes said, 'It's you again, you sleazebag. I hope you aren't going to waste my precious time. I have three mouths to feed. You wouldn't understand my values. You're a disease the politicians ignore'. Karl was too taut and tensed up to care. He tossed the stone onto the shop's armoured glass counter. The old man remained impassive. He only did business with Karl because Karl's father was in the can. He felt sorry for Karl's mother who was friends with his wife. He and Karl had a mutual loathing for each other. But they needed one another.

'Gotta be worth twenty,' Karl said as he wretched inwardly.

'What do you know, punk?' The old man paid hush money to

Massa Charlie, so he had no fear of Karl. And Karl knew it. Karl's eyes could hold on to the old man's.

'Ten.'

'Fifteen at least! I could take it elsewhere,' Karl grimaced.

'But you won't, punk, because you need to be high and the hour's journey would send you cold turkey!' The old man's sister had been an addict who had turned to religion and underneath his bravado he felt sorry for the two-bit kid from his neighbourhood. Really he did.

'Fifteen, old man, or I'll tell Charlie.' It was an empty threat and the two knew it. But street-cred honour had to be seen to be worked out. They were old adversaries. Karl usually came to the old man when there was no other way out and he was too strung out to rob somebody.

'Ten.'

Karl smashed his fists on the strong glass and sweat flowed from his forehead onto the surface. He was desperate, but still able to summon up his macho persona in front of the old man. He had his pride after all. He nodded helplessly. More sweat hit the armoured glass top. The old man turned his back on Karl. He opened a small safe behind the counter and took out a ten pound note. He'd been robbed so much before Massa Charlie gave him protection that it was a matter of habit, keeping everything in the safe. Then he gestured to Karl, who put the stone between them onto the counter. The old man took it and placed the note into the boy's hand. Then he put the stone nonchalantly into his safe. Karl fled for his fix at top speed.

The old man flipped the closed sign on his door and locked up. It was five-thirty local time. It had been a hard day. He'd have whisky in the jar tonight, the stone could wait. He'd ring Diamond Jim in the morning.

Later, the old man sat in companionable silence with his sister. He'd lived with her for the past five years since his precious wife had died of cancer. The old man lived for whisky and the bottle lived with the old man. He always offered Elsbeth, his sister, something but she always refused, snorting indignantly at him because it was against her faith. She went to church three times a week round the corner but she took care of the old man as no wife could. They loved each other dearly. She'd given up on him in terms of the Lord. But she and the brethren at the church prayed for him emotionally and violently. They still wanted him to come to church. He never went. Faith to the old man was personal. Not something you wailed about. He had no time for what he termed the 'Glory Hallelujah set'. Though he secretly respected them and always lifted his cap to the young born-again pastor. The old man hedged his bets. He'd seen too much of life to trust in a benevolent God. But he believed in his own way. He was never superstitious like the voodoo crowd across the road. He'd given them a wide berth, ever since the High Priest's daughter had fondled him in his shop hoping to get his compliance. The old man had dined out on it for a long time but he knew the voodoo people too well to have reciprocated. The voodoo people 'lost' others for less. No. He kept his own counsel. But, in his own way, he believed – though he'd never admit it to his sister.

The old man had run with Diamond Jim before Jim had joined the mob and got promoted. Financially and socially Jim was out of the old man's league. He had a brand new convertible, a station wagon and a house in Monterey. Jim was different. He was ruthless, was Jim. He'd always been that way when they'd fought in the old village before it had been torn down. Jim was upwardly mobile. He spoke and people were wasted. To all the young punks Diamond Jim was 'the Man'. He had a fistful of gold rings, bracelets, and a gold chain around his neck. And on his arm he had the tattoo that scared them off. Jim just needed to sit down at a restaurant and roll up his shirt sleeves for there to be a reaction. The sign of his Triad-esque tattoo had them obeying his every whim. Yes, Diamond Jim knew his business. He was good at spotting antiques, especially jewellery. *Jim would know*, the old man thought, resolving to ring him tomorrow. The old man knew Jim had cash in his pocket and that if he paid his dues Diamond Jim would see he was protected. Jim and he went back a few years.

Jim had gone up in the world. He moved with the times. He was the future. The old man was the past. It was the way of the world, as old as the ark. When they were young the old man had the chance of riding with the Wild Boys as Jim had done. But he'd married a God-fearing woman who hadn't wanted that for her husband. Still, he'd been happy. And he'd been able to sleep nights. No addicts or gambling for him, Leave that to the 'Flyboys'! They knew the odds. In Jim's world only the fittest survived. And Jim was especially good at that, having the intelligence of a rattlesnake. He had no enemies. He was a good contact to have in a poor neighbourhood. That's why the old man slept in peace.

'It's me.' He gave no name. They knew each other's voices. He'd got through to the minder straight away. The man had been told by Diamond Jim always to put the old man through. He obeyed his keeper.

'Old friend. How's tricks?'

'Got something up your street. Out of my league, Jimbo.' He used the old nickname and both relaxed even though they sometimes went years without talking.

'OK. I'll drop by today. Shalom.'

Jim was a devout family man and part Jewish. His son had had his Bar Mitzvah and he had two more children – though one was a girl. Jim didn't like girls for kids, but he put up with her. He had hopes that his eldest son would be a lawyer or an accountant or even better, a politician. It was early days, but Jim was ambitious for Levi.

The reason for Jim's closeness to the old man was simple: a long time ago the old man had saved Jim's life. A rival gang had put a contract out on Diamond Jim and the old man tipped him off where and when the hit was about to take place. After that Jim always visited the old man *tout de suite*.

The swanky black Jaguar purred along the road. The minder turned the engine off and let Diamond Jim out.

'I'll be back in fifteen minutes.'

The driver smiled assurance. Jim went in.

Meanwhile, Karl was elated. The pang of physical hunger inside him drove him on. And on and on. He short circuited some streets by cutting over through gardens, terrorising local cats as he did so. It took him seven minutes if he ran and fifteen minutes walking. Today he ran. The blood in his veins pumped power-fully. He felt pain in the centre of his stomach. His hands shook involuntarily. He began to fantasise as he went. He saw himself riding on horseback to rescue Snow from her captors. Snow was his pusher. And amazingly she was female. She had cornered the market in this neighbourhood for gear. Secretly Karl admired her curves and felt a conflicting combination of grown up feelings mixed with puppyish adoration for her. He hadn't really worked it out. She'd taken heroin for twelve years before breaking the habit and working as Massa Charlie's pusher. She was as lethal as a barracuda, but had a sort of fatal beauty. Her black leather jacket was too large and her jeans were crease-tight around the crotch. She behaved inconsistently towards her users, favouring them when they bought from her and treating them like dirt when they had no cash. He had seen her lose her temper with a female junkie. It had taken her fifteen seconds to garrotte the girl. Karl gave her respect.

He knocked on the rusty old door bearing the number twenty-two.

Snow looked out of the first floor window. The door opened for him. She smiled her enigmatic smile. He was in luck, she seemed in a good mood. He climbed the uncarpeted stairs; a picture of Che Guevara looked down at him. When he got to Snow's lounge she made a theatrical bow and pursed her fingers in the gesture demanding payment. Karl nodded. He gave her the tenner. There was dry sweat on the note. Snow seemed to take ages to decide whether it was OK or not. Then she pocketed the money in her creased jeans, and went to a drawer to Karl's left. This ceremony differed every time Karl visited her. Sometimes it was under the table, sometimes on top of the wall unit. At other times it was in the cupboards. Snow was a pro. She didn't take chances with her punters, for each was capable of violence. If they couldn't find the deadly powder they couldn't rob her. Snow did business better than any man, Karl thought. That's why she did what she did. Karl felt the feeling similar to bloodlust in his emotions. He liked this feeling. His body was cranked up but his spirit was free. Snow smiled. Maliciously she gleamed and the gap between her teeth where she'd been beaten opened at Karl. He stayed motionless, transfixed by the little ceremony that Snow was performing. The room was gaudily furnished with last year's carpets and throw over chairs that you disappeared into. Snow rounded an occasional table. She took a spoon and put some of the white powder in it then she lit it underneath with a match. Next she put some tobacco into a roll-up paper. It was see-through. When the 'H' was crisp and hot she decanted it into the cigarette paper. Without speaking she handed the cigarette to Karl along with the phial of white substance. Karl lit the home-made cigarette. That was all he remembered. Next was endless sleep.

Until the next time.

Diamond Jim entered the old man's shop. He remembered how he had first bought it over thirty years ago. The neighbourhood was curt and crisp and the tone of the place was respectable in those days. Now people had to detour to visit the shop. It was in the middle of bedsit land. The demolition tractors were in the neighbouring village. Tim realised that when the old man hung up his guns the shop would go with him. The old man had a reputation for old-world uprightness and dignity. People made detours to visit him. He had built up their goodwill over the years. He treated people with old-fashioned respect. Everyone was important to the old man. Even the children who dared each other to ring his bell when he was in the back. It was a pity that the old man hadn't a son, thought Jim as he walked in breezily. The old man saw him and reached for the teapot. Jim knew better than to refuse. He would spin it out, this one source of power which he had over his influential friend.

'Ça va?'

'Hmmm. You look good,' came the reply.

There was an expectant silence for Jim knew the old man never summoned him for a trifle. *This must be important*, he pondered. He feigned impatience and so the old man kept him waiting until the tea boiled. He poured the most beautiful Earl Grey tea. He had always had the most exquisite taste in tea. Jim savoured a gulp and he began to remember how much this old soldier had meant to him and how he had neglected to ensure his safety and health. Jim didn't bear him any ill-will, he just was too busy to care. The old man, however, did care. That was the difference between them. You cared and you stayed poor, you killed and you got rich. For a price. Jim had thought about this many times – especially when he had to ruthlessly exterminate a rival or an unfaithful foot soldier. He possessed what he called 'the killing madness'. Some men lusted after riches, some after women, some after power. Jim lusted after blood. He *needed* to cut men's throats. It was a pathological need deep inside him. He was and always would be an efficient serial killer. Every time he did it he felt ecstasy and peace. His high was murder, not sex or money. Jim had realised he was different when he and the old man ran with the old-fashioned teenage gangs. He remembered even now his first kill. It was a woman junkie who tried to rob him. He still to this day felt that subliminal buzz when he slit somebody's throat or carved out their innards.

He quickly earned a fearsome reputation. But he was a slave to 'the killing madness' and he knew deep inside that it would claim him one day. *But not today,* Jim thought to himself. The old man began to speak. Jim woke up from his daydream.

'Came across something yesterday.' Jim nodded.

'Never seen anything like it. Seems as though it comes from another planet if you ask me.' The old man was warming to his theme. Jim was interested. The old man didn't get excited about nothing.

'So?'

'You in?'

'The usual rates, my friend. I never fail as far as poppy is concerned.' The old man smiled a contented smile. This was his moment of power and he was milking it for all it was worth. Jim knew him too well to rush him. The old man reached into his pinny and took out a large object. He held it in both hands theatrically and his tone became conspiratorial.

'It may be worth a bit to you and your contacts.' They never used names, Jim and the old man. Jim listened intently. He remembered the 'Lion of Malta' – the largest ruby in the US that the old man had caught for him from a poor woman who fell on hard times, not knowing its true value. Jim felt greed enter his stomach. A deep yearning hunger permeated his senses. He was still, after all these years, put in the old man's hands! It was a good job his foot soldiers didn't know of his vulnerability.

Then the old man placed the large object on the armour-plated counter. It was clean and free of Karl's sweaty imprint. The old man was fastidious in his old-worldly cleanliness. He cleaned at five every morning from room to room. Today was no different. Jim saw the object for the first time. It was a muddy, earthy colour, large in size as stones go. It could have been a stone caked in mud. But Jim knew better. It was too large for a diamond. It could be topaz, or even an aquamarine. Jim never made quick judgements. Life was seldom pure and rarely simple. The truth was often hard to find and when discovered, different to its surface value. Jim picked the stone up.

It was heavy.

Their eyes met and said, 'We've got something but it's too early to say what yet!' No words were said, but you could cut the atmosphere with a knife. Both men remained companionably silent.

Finally Jim said, 'I'll get our contacts to clean it. Discover what it is. Then we'll have Sotheby's value it in our business antiques front!'

The old man nodded meaningfully. He took a piece of white used cloth and wrapped up the gem in it. He handed it to Jim. They trusted one another implicitly. If it was valuable Jim would see to it that the old man received his commission.

'By the way, how's your sister?' Jim enquired.

'OK,' came the economic reply. They shook hands and Jim walked out to his car where his driver feigned attentiveness and disguised wear and tear.

Another day, another dollar, thought Jim.

'There but for the Grace of God...' the old man smiled.

The thick-set balding man took a puff of his cigar, waited momentarily for the effect and then blew smoke rings into the already smoke-drenched room. Silence pervaded the atmosphere.

Diamond Jim stood facing the beautifully ugly man – almost at attention. Jim had a tense expression on his face. He waited for the words to enter the stratosphere. No one sat in his presence.

Silence.

Another inhalation on the cigar.

Horatio Hopkins – or HH to his friends and enemies alike – dined out on his sense of timing. He could have taught the great Frank Sinatra about timing. He was wearing a Hector Powe brown check suit – not too loud but definitely a parody of what people wore in the cities of commerce. It was truly brown with green checks on it. HH was the doyen of bad taste and liked it that way. The glass-topped Italian table looked out into the long ostentatiously decorated room. The gold piping of the table's frame bent double. It was architecturally a work of art and was a personal present from the Sultan of Brunei's nephew.

Hopkins finally spoke. 'Jim,' he said, 'I'm worried.'

Jim's back arched and the muscles on his legs tensed up subconsciously. He knew fear. The euphemism of 'concern' meant that the big man had information that at best, was not good.

Jim waited. The atmosphere wailed with unsaid feeling. Jim wanted the floor to open up. More silence.

'I was dining with the VP the other month', he continued, 'and he was worried about a rape in your neck of the woods. He said he had his best men on it. The leads went to your soldiers, and he told me to put it right!'

'Yes, HH.' Jim remembered the splay of the girl's panties, the ripping sound as he had torn her undergarments off her. He recalled the beads of sweat on her black temples and the animal fear she exuded. It had been an exceptionally brutal act and an example of Jim's need to terrorise and maim people for life. His Jekyll and Hyde existence had got him into trouble. The girl had been a school teacher who coached at the local university and there had been political backlash over the attack, especially from the Principal of New Falls university. The Principal played golf with the Vice President of the United States. He always lost to the VP but this time one of his protégés had been the victim.

The police hadn't exactly endeared themselves to the girl and on the following Monday morning an identikit photograph drawing was highlighted in the New York Tribune's third page. They got everything right with the exception of Jim's eyes. Jim's eyes spoke volumes. They were Bambi-like and spoke a thousand sonatas; women and men loved his eyes. They were come-to-bed eyes to women and plausible 'come up and get me' eyes to his own sex. Because the eyes were normal – whatever that meant – Jim escaped with an identity parade scare. He was free but the police were highly suspicious. Nothing had stood. The girl had purple panties with a black bra. She'd been playing badminton in the recreation hall and for Jim the 'killing madness' had come upon him. As always, Jim was remorseful and sorry, so that didn't make him a psychopath. Just amoral. The girl was a sculptural he-woman with rippling muscles who'd put up a good fight. Jim had a clawed back which no-one knew about. Thank God.

The VP had leant on HH and HH was making his presence felt.

'I don't want to moralise. But I've groomed you for my successor and I don't want to be proved wrong. You have one fault and there it is. What have you got to say, Diamond Jim?'

When he used his full name, Jim knew that his boss was truly angry. Jim had put the three-carat diamond into the gap in his teeth just for HH's benefit. He knew this would be difficult to call. HH had trained him from a boy. The layers of fat undulated out of HH's short-cut fully starched collar. It made him seem to be bigger than he was. In fact, during HH's youth he had played as a prop in the England 'A' Rugby team under Jeff Cooke's regime. A serious injury to his right eye – the result of an off-the-ball incident – had finished HH's playing career. It was a shame because he had the potential to go the whole way. He was even rumoured by the sages to be a future England Captain. He still sat at the best seats at Twickenham and to all and sundry he was a tough but genuine businessman. But he had taken a bribe and he was a *Cosa Nostra* man through and through. He spearheaded the family's legal division. He was a new type of criminal conversant with computer hacking and high octane fraud. His flesh was red with too much wine – he drank two bottles of *Rose d'Anjou* a day – and he could have been mistaken for Father Christmas.

But he ruled with an iron fist. Whenever he became worried it meant trouble for the participant.

'I'm taking you off the Miami side and giving it to Lyle to troubleshoot. You will report to me daily at 1000 hours without fail until further notice.' Lyle was HH's watchdog, short, fat, slimy and untrustworthy. He resembled a Doberman pinscher watchdog and he ferreted around discovering skeletons in people's cupboards. No one was immune. Definitely not Jim.

Jim sighed. 'You're the boss, my father.'

'I'm your boss, my son.'

The serious religious words were a sign of the love covenant between the two men. Jim hoped that he'd be put out of sight until the high profile rape disappeared from view. The decision had been made for him. Despite all his experiences, Diamond Jim had felt uneasy in the street when he'd come across patrolmen in the last few weeks. He'd been on the run before and he'd never lost the frantic paranoia that such an experience gave a person. The big man nodded. The two chunky minders motioned Jim to the door twenty feet away and Jim was sandwiched between them.

'How are you, Manolo?' Jim enquired.

'Beware, *hombre*,' came the menacing reply. If a contract was to be put out, Manolo had twenty-nine kills under his belt and Jim would take him to the big 3-0. He couldn't afford to get personal. Like Jim, death was a way of life for him and he kept HH's orders to the letter.

Jim shivered and shrugged more manfully than he felt and they parted. Jim's minder looked apprehensively at his boss. He looked into those big brown eyes and saw fear. He said nothing. He knew Jim too well to cross him. He opened the door for Jim who entered the car, slinking in like an anaconda with strongly toned markings over his slimy skin. The driver got in.

'Take me to my office'.

Once ensconced in the desk, he made a call to Sotheby's. To Major Thruxton-Smith, late of the Royal Marines, Sandhurst and Dartmouth. A marine and soldier all in one.

'I'm sending you a circular of a stone I want you to value, Major,' Jim snapped.

The Major stood to attention in his voice, 'Yes Sir.'

'I'll bring it personally on Friday. Shall we say eleven?'

'I'll have some coffee ready, Sir. I await your instructions.'

Jim knew of three men in the world who understood the gem

scene as well as the Major. He used the Major very rarely as gems were his department under the legitimate arm of the family's tentacles. The Major and he went back five years, long enough to be chums. They needed one another. They never actually dropped their guard but they held one another in mutual respect. The Major always spoiled him when he came to the Smoke. Like many a true soldier the Major was good at carrying out orders. His was not to reason why, but to do or die. The Major was a good Lieutenant to Jim. He never had got promoted during his military career because he didn't suffer the foolish half-Colonels gladly. Plus the fact that his Sandhurst career had been broken off at the outbreak of the Mau Mau crisis in Kenya in the '50s. Still he was a good man to have on your team. And his expertise was highly prized all over the whole world. The Major was a Sotheby's man through and through.

'Book me a one-way ticket to Heathrow on Thursday afternoon, Jean,' he barked to his secretary. 'Book me a suite at the Inn on the Park for the weekend.' Then he turned his settee into a bed and slept uneasily; tossing over in his mind for a full and long three hours. The stone would redeem him, Jim smiled to himself. He hated the waiting.

The supersonic aircraft taxied along Heathrow's number three runway at 1730 hours London time. Jim had lost a few hours. He felt it. When he was young he could take the pace. Now at forty-eight, he felt it.

The Major stood with the crowd awaiting all those from the trans-Atlantic flight. Jim poked at his umpteenth grey leather wallet – a present for all passengers on Concorde. He slipped it into a side pocket and those eyes smiled at the Major.

'Nice of you to come, Major.'

'We aim to please, Sir.'

'Inn on the Park and some tea. Then I'll fill you in.'

'Rightey-ho, Sir,'

They lapsed into companionable silence as the company car, a Vauxhall Vector, trawled through the traffic madness that is London town. They travelled slowly through Piccadilly, decked out with addicts and people, into the Mayfair. The car stopped. They walked slowly over a patch of green which was verdant at this time of year. When they had checked in at the plush hotel, Jim afforded him a smile.

'I have on my person something of interest to you, Major.'

'Do tell.'

'It's not like anything I've come across before and I knew you'd be able to give me an expert opinion.'

'If it's a mined on earth, I'll place it for you, Mr Kennedy,' the major retorted. The violinist in the hotel lounge merged into 'O Sole Mio', and Jim began to get excited. Jewels excited Jim. Some men loved horses, others antiques, some were into paintings, and yet others loved beautifully constructed buildings.

But Jim loved Jewels. His babies, he'd affectionately call them. He had an eye for value. This stone got him excited – he felt it could be really famous.

Patiently he unfolded the white dirty cloth out onto the table and looked straight into the Major's eyes. Jim liked eye contact. He had the Major's attention. His eyes shined like dark rubies; the Major was under his spell.

He opened the wrapping and theatrically picked up the largish stone with his right hand.

The Major was inscrutable. He sighed. He looked at the stone for a long time. Jim held his gaze, a king in the man's short legs, thick torso and ape-like shoulders. He drank in the man's tweed jacket and checked country shirt and plain tie. The cavalry twilled slacks were exquisitely pressed. If the Major did anything he did it well.

He looked up at Jim.

'This stone is honed and mined deep in the east. I'd have to take it and do tests on it but I believe it is a new type only found deep in the centre of the ocean. There is a legend that when men mine these stones the rivers will be filled with blood.'

Jim was interested. His instincts, as always, were being proved right; this would redeem him in HH's opinion.

'What sort of rivers of blood, my military friend?'

'It is an old Polynesian tale,' said the Major. 'And it talks of a paradise under the seabed. The type men would die for. It goes on about mermen and mermaids, who are a race Hitler might have dreamt of and who hold supernatural power in their persons.

Legend has it that they inhabited Greenland but that when colonial settlers and Eskimos moved in they fled to a special city deep under the seabed. They hold powers to bewitch polar bears and whales instinctively. They possess great power but they are wary of using it in the presence of their war-like cousins. The legend has never been proven by the Polynesians but they believe this and some own up to having had experience with these people.'

'Take me to someone who has met such people. Keep the stone for tests, give me a receipt and my time is yours.'

'It would be a pleasure, Sir. In fact I know someone here in London who might talk to you. But there is a condition.'

'Yes?'

'He's a cripple. Tells some tale of a magic curse which shrivelled up his arms. His arms are half-length. Still, he may talk to you. He lives on a houseboat on the Thames. I'll give him a call.'

'This will be a pleasure,' said Jim. 'Dare we break up the day in celebration? Brandy, Major? It's not everyday that we find a pearl beyond price.'

'There's one condition, Sir.'

'Oh?'

'You have got to have faith to believe this legend. It is only told to those who trust in the impossible.'

'I am beginning to believe, Major,' Jim purred. 'I'm beginning to be a believer.'

The two men lapsed into companionable silence. The violinist played 'The Streets of London'.

Chapter Two

This was New York City and it was hot. The smoke filled the room. It was a cavern. It had a ghostly presence to it. There was a Chesterfield settee along the side of the room with a green Dralon ruche-sided chair. Very comfortable in a masculine way. Adorning the length of the room was a Baroque mirror with gilt rims along its bottom. On a side table sat a tasteful nude ballet performer incorporating a light. Incongruously there were videos strewn around on top of each other and betting slips all over the tables at the side of the upholstered furniture. Suddenly something moved. Inside the room a figure glided into the kitchen. He was short, 5'8" at the most, lion-sized with tight buttocks. A cigarette dangled from his mouth. He was obviously nervous. Gliding along like some demented wildcat. He paced the floor like a black panther. His face was lived in with eyes that smiled at you with a sort of spirited luminosity. They lit the room; they were soft but strong.

He was as nervous as a cat on hot bricks. His eyes spoke into the dark room.

They weren't earthly eyes. They belonged to some distant land where spiritual values ruled. They penetrated and overruled human contact. It took a strong man to challenge their gaze. They asked too many questions. And they rested awhile until the person looked at reacted in one way or another. He drank another instant cup of coffee and lit his umpteenth cigarette, and the haze of cigarette smoke drenched his clothes. He was waiting; whatever he was waiting for was important. He picked up his empty cigarette packet and threw it in the bin, then the bell went. He jumped rigidly to attention – with a garish intensity.

The bell rang a second time. And a third; there was silence, the man did nothing.

He faced the ground, then he dragged himself up, hitched up his jeans and slid into the hall, opening the door with an easy action, his eyes sparkling as they glared luminously at his visitors.

The two men came in.

'They must believe...' he muttered to himself. His eyes met the strangers in thought. He looked through them both. Then, as if having made up his mind, he opened the door wide. He possessed style. The two strangers were all eyes – aware that they were being submitted to some pagan test.

Silence hung in the air. He motioned them both to chairs. They sat, accomplices to the mood of the moment. The Major had warned Diamond Jim that this man was unreliable; he was some sort of prophet who listened with his inner ear. Jim was visibly overawed. He felt a sort of giddy presence which made him light-headed and dizzy. He had not experienced this sort of thing before. He was a man of power, used to taking charge. In the time they took to settle, Jim felt out of control. He felt almost drunk and he didn't like to be out of control.

The Major broke the ice. 'We've come to learn about your people. About the legend of the stone and all you want to tell us about. It seems trite, but we come in spirit and in peace.'

The bright eyes blinked; was there a tear in them? The Major could only guess.

'There is a story that the queen of our peoples will meet a prince of the peoples of the earth. Together they will fuse our peoples so that we can come out from our hidden home. Then the rivers of blood will flow and white will become black and black, white!'

'What does this mean?' Jim enquired.

'Our time is near. I can feel it in my spirit. We march to the drum of time that you cannot hear.'

'Why not?'

'Because you need to listen to the spirit!'

'What spirit?'

'He will tell you all things.'

'You speak in riddles.'

'I prophesise the truth. In my land I was a prophet. Then I made a pact with the dark side and I bear on my body the marks of our creator's wrath...'

'I see.'

'The interview is over. You will not believe. I have nothing more to say to you. Go in peace.' The eyes danced with aggression across the two men's faces. Jim felt sick inside. He sensed a presence. Time seemed to stand still. He wanted to learn more of this cripple. But he knew he was out of his depth.

'Thank you, friend,' he muttered as the bright eyes ushered him out.

The sun set across the New York skyline. The city sleeps. The bright eyes stayed alive for a long time.

Kayley wheeled herself along the sidewalk. It was New York in September, and the chill in the air reminded her of London, and how she's once loved to wheel along Wimbledon Common and through Regent's Park. She loved London. Paris she knew and Rome she respected, but London had belonged to her. She had spent three years there, and had lived in a two-up, two-down in Chelsea.

Yet in the world's eyes she was a cripple. Someone who had to use a wheelchair. A half-person. She was the proprietor of a magazine charting the evidence of UFOs and the paranormal. It was hard to publish this monthly magazine but Kayley was good at her job, and she did not suffer fools gladly. She'd arrived a little like the prophet Elijah in the Old Testament, suddenly coming onto the scene and telling King Ahab that it wouldn't rain for three and a half years.

She had arrived in London like some meteor across the night skies. She was a breath of fresh air to all she came into contact with. Her eyes were exceptional. They shone like beacons in a cold dull sky. It was as if she didn't need her other limbs. Her face was classically Grecian. She had a strong nose with full lips. She possessed a type of beauty that seemed to break all the rules. Nothing was exactly right. More importantly, her voice had a rich velvet pitch that was hypnotic. She did not speak of her disability. She sought no pity and expected no concessions at all. 'I am a woman of many moods and born of many seasons,' she would say to anyone who sought some sort of understanding. Being disabled was not what she saw herself as. She was without bitterness or resentment. She rarely had a temper but when she did she really let rip, and folk had to watch out. When people met Kayley they were hypnotised by her eyes. They spoke of a million things. They had a language all of their own as if she came from somewhere unearthly. Her clothes were standard. Power dressing was her penchant and she was partial to sculptural brooches and kaleidoscopic earrings. Her underlings deferentially called her 'The Countess'. She was wheeling her way to a press conference about a new publication on world religions and philosophies, and their connection to the unexplained.

Kayley spent every night in her own personalised golden bath with the letter 'K' engraved on the bottom. She needed to spend from midnight to dawn in the water to charge up her batteries because she was a waterling and belonged to the world under the sea. Her fellow men and women were a super-intelligent race who had quelled violence and war and lived beneath the surface. They were a peace-loving race and had embraced the harmonious. They evolved from one human family who escaped and lived in a bubble at the bottom of the sea when the last Ice Age occurred.

They learned to be self-sufficient and as generations passed they grew the grey fins and scaly tails. However, they possessed the abilities of the humanoids and the ability to speak in whatever language was required, hence Kayley's ability to speak fluent English. Every evening at six Kayley telepathically contacted her teacher, the learned Amos, who is a bearded merman. Men taught women and women taught men in their world. She told Amos last night that he needed to turn up the iron input in her body as she was getting extra tired.

She is celibate. In her world she is a princess of the vestal virgin warrior queens who guard the royal personages of the line of rulers in Atlantis. Because they have eliminated war, the people live long lives. Kayley herself is 201 years old. However, if Kayley chose to forsake her role of princess and mate with anyone whatsoever, her supernatural powers would be lost and another woman would become Princess of Atlantis. And Kayley would revert to a normal lifespan – aging, for Atlanteans is a result of missing the spiritual mark.

Because they live long, they put themselves to sleep at the

maximum age of 250. This has been decided in the 'Judicium', the board of overseers for the city of Atlantis. The members of the Judicium are called from the tribe of descendants that originated in the original family. There are twelve of them and a chairperson who casts the deciding vote when the company cannot agree. The members of the Judicium are permitted for the sake of the continuation of the race, to live for 500 years.

They have a method of putting one another to sleep. The law was passed 600 years previously that at the age of 250 the son would do the honour of terminating the life of his father or mother. One of the qualities of the Judicium is honesty, which is revered as a god-like quality. As we humans revere holiness so do the Atlanteans honour truthfulness. The more truthful you are the more supernatural power you possess and the longer you live. Justus I was the first King of Atlantis. He reigned 6,000 years ago. It was he who built the city's protective armour-plated glass and he who created the kingship in the Kingdom. He grappled with Rustum the Terrible who terrorised and raped the people. Justus and Rustum were brothers. Justus was two years older than Rustum. But Rustum was a deceiver and a cheat. He was a fleshy bisexual male vamp; he thrived on killing. Because of the war to the death between Justus and Rustum with swords, Justus was badly wounded – near fatally. Honor was the person who nursed him back to life. She had incredible healing powers. She stayed awake for thirty days nursing him. She possessed the ability to sleep on her feet so she didn't fade and die. She married Justus and their child, Omorc, became the first princess of the Atlanteans. Her brother Rory was the person who quelled the warrior instinct in those from Atlantis. Rory ruled for a thousand years. This was a time of harmony and peace. The people born in his time became the harmonious people. Atlantis was now thirty thousand years old. It had become curious of 'the world beyond the sea' so Kayley was sent up to view matters above the water. She resided in New York now, in a luxury mansion in Staten Island, with immense super-intelligent security which seemed to be impenetrable to earthlings. Because she reported the progress of the worldlings, she had to have the cover of a job.

To run her own newspaper was a good cover – especially as

she had a keen perception of the unexplained. She fitted in well and was a socialite at a time when disabled people were becoming accepted by most of the American upper classes. She had a helper, her general manager Judy, who was a humanoid who suspected Kayley's supernatural powers but chose to keep her feelings to herself. Kayley chose to keep her own counsel and Judy was indeed open to bribes, for the right price. It was a bit like Jesus and Judas, potentially Kayley realised that Judy was a good general manager however, and respected her knowledge of the earthlings' customs.

Judy had set up the press conference. They were floating the sister paper to the public and they were highlighting the 'Texas nightmare experience' as their lead story. This was the story of Dan and Annette Page who had been abducted. Annette claimed she had been raped by seven extra-terrestrials whilst Dan had had to watch. The aliens had been white with slinky cat's eyes. Siamese cats. It was six months since the abduction. Dan and Annette had been discovered in the Utah Flats near Salt Lake City. They had been fed and watered and had lived on wild locusts and honey. Despite their ordeal they had been none the worse for wear physically. Kayley had bought the rights to the story and the press conference had the rights to go public.

Kayley was excited because earthlings, with the imminent arrival of the millennium, were particularly interested in the supernatural. After the press conference there was a cocktail party at Trump Towers with everybody who was anybody being invited. People with influence and money felt comfortable with Kayley because she possessed the unique grace of those who are truly great.

The conference was set for noon. Dan and Annette were edgy. Kayley used Dr Hans Andersen, a lion of a man, a gentle giant who possessed an acutely good bedside manner. Dr Andersen was a Nobel Prize winner and was of Scandinavian descent. Kayley and he revelled in true honesty and understood each other well. He worked for Kayley on a commission-only basis which went to his trust, 'The Andersen Trust', largely because he earned so much that it made more sense to give money to charity than be a target for the taxman.

Kayley had let it be known by quiet assumption that she had been paralysed from the waist down from birth. Dr Andersen was her confidant and although she did not make him privy to her innermost secrets, she had her eye on him. He had passed her tests and, being a person of worldwide renown, was largely not open to bribes.

The press had flocked to the conference. Dan and Annette, dressed in sober clothes, sat at the centre. Kayley was to their right and Judy took the place with the public relations company. She had interests in the PR company and as a favour to Kayley was handling the matter herself.

Still, she was not entirely trustworthy but Kayley admired her workman-like ability to get the most out of a situation. If it could be milked, Judy would milk it.

The conference warmed up with a few non-committal statements from non-inflammatory people. Then Percy Goldblum spoke up. 'How do we take this? There is no proof and the Pages could be mounting a giant hoax.'

Judy countered excellently. 'Indulge your readers – allow them to judge the accounts of Mr and Mr Page for themselves. I will allow you to interview them for fifteen minutes after both have spoken, as a token of my evaluation of the seriousness of the subject.'

With that, Dan sat up. He spoke poignantly. He didn't use any posh words and his description was riveting in its economy. He sat down and Annette then spoke. Choked and upset, her diction was suspect, but the conference, even at that point, was surely a rip-roaring success. There could be a battalion of Percy Goldblums after this and they still would be won over. Judy clutched Kayley's hand as women do. Kayley smiled back. Now for the cocktail party.

Trump Tower was gorgeous in its ostentation. Donald Trump could be seen amongst the marble and gold if you looked hard enough. A bold, powerfully built man with a brash presence, he epitomised the American Dream.

Ju-jube McGovern escorted her as he always did. He was a handsome man with a withered hand. He was classless and Kayley loved him dearly in a childlike soul-brother way. They chatted gaily throughout the proceedings.

Steven sat down. This was a great honour to sit down at Jackson's Club in the centre of Mayfair.

Steven was compact with thick-set muscular arms, and a lean stomach. He was forty-two. His age and experience gave him the edge over other more foolhardy people. He was 5'11", dark-haired with blue eyes which turned green when he was riled. He walked with a limp; a wound of war given to him by Horatio Hopkins in his days with the service. Hopkins had spared his life when he had been discovered at the centre of the Cosa Nostra's operations. It was out of character for Hopkins. Steve believed that the spear on the wall that he had thrown had missed. But it had hit his ankle and Steve had spent three months in hospital whilst they had argued his case, the physicians wanting to cure by medication and the surgeons preferring to do damage by the knife. In the end Steve had implored them to operate. A tense five-hour operation had taken place. They had saved the leg but he would forever be crippled, as he put it. A wound to forever remind him of war.

He was invalided out of the Secret Service and he now ran his own mercenary company with considerable success seeing that he had successfully protected Wilson from an assassin's gun. He was in demand. Steve was a perfectionist, and he didn't allow personal relationships to affect his devotion to duty. Of course, he had had many chances but in all things professional, Steve did not fail. He would have made a good priest. A gun-toting Holy Joe. Steve smiled as he made small talk with Jackson's son-in-law, Peter Lawson. The two liked each other and their paths met very rarely now. They insulted each other shamelessly and were a match for each other at the snooker table. If Steve was lucky he would avenge himself tonight, he thought. Lawson was like a Greek god. Blonde, even-bodied, blue-eyed, white complexion. He was used to being admired and this narcissism was one of his faults. Used to being the centre of attention, he was also dramatic and a mean shot at big-game hunting. The two men had spent prime time shooting big game in Africa. So Steve was conversant with the African situation, especially in South Africa where Mandela had achieved saint-like status.

Yet a spectre loomed over South Africa. Mandela's Vice President was known to have had ties with the Chinese Triads. He'd become respectable, as they all tended to do. Odinga Odinga was a rat. He had maimed, killed and massacred many whites and Mandela had positioned him in this place purely for political ends. Steve had met Mandela and like others had been impressed not with his presence, so much, but by his warmth. Shortly after his experience, Steve had gone to find solace in a Tibetan monastery in Sri Lanka, affiliated with Buddhist monks. Life was important to Steve now. He had come to terms with his mercenary leanings; he loved the buzz of the assassin. But Steve had a conscience.

He had remembered the day when one of Odinga's jackals had killed his fiancée, Diamond Ludwig. She was from Liechtenstein and had been a semi-professional skier taking part in the Olympics. Steve's job had been to protect the British PM at the games and he had met Diamond in a drunken mess at the end of his tour. The PM had gone home and Steve had let himself loose on Kandersteg in Switzerland. Diamond, for her part, had been happy until forced to become engaged to a millionaire's son who was the personification of boredom. As a devoted daughter of her monied father, she was sure to be faithful to her matched liaison. Then she met her mad-holy man. Steve, not knowing who she was, had been drawn to her long blonde locks and the ample proportions of her curves, which seemed to go on forever. They had been in the same club when DD, her fiancé, had got into a fight with Steve's friends. In the way of the true warrior, Steve eschewed violence. He had disarmed DD of his broken bottle and returned him to his chalet. Diamond gave him her card. The atmosphere had been electric, even in Steve's drunken state. Diamond fell fully in love with him and called off her engagement. However, Steve was not considered the right material and they had been forbidden to meet again. But Steve was a one-woman guy. Then Diamond had been taken hostage by a triad gang for money. Her father, a ruthless businessman, had been short of paying and Diamond was killed in a deadly shoot-out. The offending people were at large and Steve had a broken heart. That was not allowed in the service and Steve was discharged from it forthwith. In the recent honour list he had been accorded an OBE. This he received with pride, being very patriotic and a devotee of all things British. Lomas had succeeded him as Chief of Operations at Downing Street, and so Steve wondered why Jackson had invited him to dinner at his club.

The Defence Minister of the South African parliament was there and Steve knew that he had been called in for a purpose. Jackson had many tricks. He had an astute brain. This brain had protected Steve on many occasions. And he was that rare commodity; a soldier who was also a statesman. Jackson had seen due at Dunkirk and El Alamein, and he was a stickler for discipline. He was called Sir Rufus Jackson in full and he, like Steve, shared a love for all things British. The pair had been like father and son and, for all his diplomatic posturing, Sir Rufus had felt weak at the knees when he had invalided Steve out of the service.

'Go with God, laddie,' he'd said. And Steve took him at his word. 'Perhaps the only person who can serve you is a Catholic Priest,' had been his advice also. Steve hadn't gone to the church but had turned to Buddhism where his warrior side was accepted and he wasn't lampooned for 'sin'. He had many, many times found peace with himself in a God whom he never dared to mention to his ex-cronies. It wasn't cricket, he thought.

'Minister, permit me to introduce you to Steven Galloway, an ex-colleague of mine and an expert in African affairs,' said Jackson. This was praise indeed and Steve eyed Jackson with suspicion which the older man observed with amusement. The men reached back into the wide Chesterfield and high-backed wing chairs that were standard issue for a Grosvenor Place men's club. The cigars were out and the port passed from man to man. Steve was not drunk. He was listening. His life had been saved by his dislike of alcohol. He drank wine and enjoyed *Château Neuf du Pape* with the best of them. But this was important and everything about his ears and eyes was ready. He knew Sir Rufus would camp it up, and wait till the last moment for his *pièce de résistance*. He was not wrong. A long time passed and several also-rans made their excuses. Then Sir Rufus straightened himself up. There were present: Sir Rufus, the Cabinet Minister, his minder, a quiet thick-set black man, Lawson and Steve.

Sir Rufus waited until the waiter took out the empties.

'Gentlemen. I have called you here to view the situation in RSA, the Minister here can fill us in on the "on-the-spot" view but it has come to our notice that a plot has been hatched to depose the government. My man in RSA has inveigled his way into a guerrilla army and they are being trained for duties over and above the normal tight schedule.' The RSA Minister nodded and as he smiled, his teeth, white as Rhino horns, lit up the room. The childlike quality of the black African was very much in evidence here.

'When and where and what we do not know. But it is evident that Odinga Odinga is tied up in it.' The Minister grunted his assent. All eyes were on Sir Rufus. No one took a swig at the port. Lawson changed position. Steve looked head-on at his former boss.

'Steven, I will talk with you tomorrow at 10 a.m. in my office. Minister, would you like to give us some ground information?'

The Minister changed. When he spoke he became a different animal. He was a leader of men. No one was immune from his power. Steven noted it down and wondered where he really stood. Did he want overall power himself? No, he was at the fount of real power and he did not possess that call to arms that the great ones did. Yet he could corrode in the coup. Steve made a mental note that the black man could not be trusted. He had an intuition as good, if not better, than most women and he was rarely wrong. He felt slightly hostile to the Minister's wares. He looked at Lawson. They exchanged glances, a nod, a smile. Lawson he could trust, or so he felt. Sir Rufus was incorruptible. He would have made an extremely good PM, but life does not always give us our just desserts. The Cabinet Minister was talking. Nothing new here, Steve observed. Then he finished.

Steve cancelled his midnight game of poker with the boys in the Wedgewood nightclub backroom. He'd pleaded a headache and the lads knew something was important. They were his family and he treated them as such. He couldn't sleep so got up to watch midnight TV. A film with Cary Grant and the semi-final first leg of the FA Cup. He was restless. Since being dismissed from the service he had learnt to move with his third eye. A clairvoyant had spoken to him about it and it had been in Sri Lanka that the monks had taught him to listen with his inner ear.

His inner ear was hearing with clarity. Something was up when he drifted off to sleep and he dreamed of someone attacking him with a dagger. The man wore a DJ and a cummerbund which was burgundy coloured and he had thick-set arms. But that was all he saw. The dream had come to him regularly and Steve knew it by heart. His sixth sense, something he did not as a soldier trust, came to him at all times. The monks in Sri Lanka had been very helpful. They believed he should be a Sahdu, an Asian holy man.

The night was cold. Nothing happened.

'The people are aware of the stone. It is in circulation but I know not how.' The caller rang off. Kayley was wide awake now. The phone positioned next to her bath had bleeped. The voice was unmistakable. He only rang when matters were important. She knew she had to fulfil her destiny. Kayley had waited for the stone to surface for many years. It had on its face the drawing of how she was to communicate in human form with the world that had sent her. All this went through her mind. She was semi-weak, it being the middle of the night, and sleep evaded her. She usually had an alarm clock to wake her at dawn. She added to the water a salt solution which kept her from cramp. Her fish-tail lay blue beneath the water, which had to be 20 per cent salt. Exactly that amount. She needed only five hours sleep at night so she spent the remaining time meditating. This corresponded with her spiritual warrior syndrome. She wrote poetry with her mind, able at all times to connect with her soul.

Every evening she put the answer phone on and retired to the basement of her house. There were seascapes and opals surrounding the bath. She had had the lounge and the dining room broken down so it was one big room. Large enough for people to be stretched out around the edges where cushions served as seats. The colour of the walls was luminous orange which was the light in her world which encouraged sleep. There was in the centre of her room a Jacuzzi-type bath. The surrounding upholstery was plain orange velvet. Pictures of mermen and mermaids done by artists from Atlantis were tastefully hung across the walls. One picture, positioned in a prime spot, was of a mermaid and a merman holding each other tightly. The man held the woman, and they were facing left as you looked at the picture. Kayley often drew strength from that picture of her ma and pa. She had lost them shortly after that picture had been taken, when she was eight. Mermaids and mermen reached majority when they were twelve. They were able to bear children much later when they were twenty-one. The time between twelve and twenty-one was a happy time in the mermaid's life, when she was free, single and safe from getting pregnant. It was the way things always had been. Kayley had been in the top 25 per cent of mermaids for intelligence. She had been hand-picked for her looks, intelligence and kinship to the human race; her sculptured bone structure gave her a Polynesian appearance and as there was a legend of the mermaids and mermen coming originally from the happy people of the Polynesian Islands, this was fitting.

This night, Kayley was excited because she knew that her destiny was to be fulfilled. She had been four years on planet earth and she had got very lonely. Flirting with people from earth only exacerbated the problem. She got broody and tended to make platonic friendships with kooky people who were unfazed by her viewpoint. To an earthling Kayley had a pleasant disposition. She had a very kind side of her nature – sought after in Atlantis – which was a compassionate gift from the great ones. Her smile won her many admirers and she was frequently propositioned by a host of people ranging from enthusiastic workmen to well-to-do diplomats. The way she played it was that she had a sick father who she had to look after. This pulled the curtain down on her relationships but inwardly Kayley yearned to love and be loved in return. She wore a type of skin-coloured brassiere, or singlet if you like, that tastefully positioned her breasts in a pointed position. She would have looked good as the sculptural headpiece of an eighteenth-century vessel. Her beauty won her many friends but she remained uncommitted to all but her cats – Burmese, whose intelligence and beauty complemented her personality and who were privy to the cavern that was her basement home. There were shells and starfish along the sides of the wall. Seamen's nets of old decked the walls and an old anchor stood above, facing Kayley. She had bought it at auction for £295 at Sotheby's in London.

Nobody except the cats came down to her subterranean cavern. They demanded little from her except feeding and there was a cat flap on the door. The basement was the nearest she could come to being at home and the closest she came in any given day to the ocean. In the daytime she wheeled in her chair for miles along the sea's edge. She loved the smell of the sea and she felt she was so near yet so far. Nobody ever guessed her secret and she had met no one to whom she could divulge her secret to.

The phone call had given her the knowledge. It was now up to her. Luckily she had an inbuilt homing device attached to her mind which made her 'sympathetic' to the stone. After all it was the type of stone that her home city was built from. Living with it gave her strength. She went to the side of her bath and sought the information she needed from her PC. It said:

> Kosmos: Sea fire energy precious stone of unknown origin. Legend has it that this stone has healing and miracle-working powers when in the hands of the warrior priestesses of the Kingdom of Atlantis, a hereditary tribe of beautiful females set apart to patrol the city and keep war to a minimum. It can be used to neutralise or disarm people in the event of war. Mining and prospecting this stone is punishable by a small fire.

She had read the dictionary's definition many times but this time she felt excitement in her veins. It was what she had been bred for, it was her destiny. Emotions she had kept in check for years now ran riot. She felt alive for the first time. And at the core of her being she felt the pull of something bigger and stronger than her. It was the pull of the sub-mariner. That was founded in her by her family when she was a child of five, when they submitted her to the warrior priestesses of Atlantis. They had spent an eternity deciding that her life was to be with them. Thereafter all she did was to live a very self-disciplined life in the army's HQ under the City of Atlantis. Only those who were blessed with upkeeping the sacred oracles of the mermaids and mermen were privy to these secrets. This was a band of mermaids who were sexless. They were a type of eunuch. They were treated with a deadly serum which took six months to debilitate all normal emotions and create a safety valve in the person so that they were sexless. These truths were her truths. They were called the Tributaries and at any one time there were always thirteen who guarded the city limits. They served the king and queen and were not obliged to declare their identities to anybody but their rulers. Their power lay in surprise. Kayley had learned early to distinguish in spirit those who were tributaries and those who were not. This was the first level for the priesthood. Once she could do that she learnt the next truths of which there were nine, the magical number for completion.

There was one particular rule – the ninth rule of the Covenant. It was that she should remain celibate for the tenure of her priesthood. If she ever cohabited with a merman she would lose her magic powers. Just like that. To her people she was a princess. The princess was subject to the king and queen. The Princess of Atlantis ruled the city for one year, thereafter she inter-reigned with the inner sanctum Privy Council. She had spent her year in Atlantis as princess and it had been a peaceful, fulfilling time. Now she shared the power of the few warrior princesses. Her commission was a responsible one. Kayley had been chosen from a shortlist of three. She had got the nod because her parents were not alive. It was considered a great honour to give yourself to such a service. She would have herself a place in Atlantean history. Hence her excitement. Slowly, Kayley let out the salty water from the bath and let down the right side so she could climb into her wheelchair to meet the world.

Chapter Three

The body lay flat on the floor. Flies were dive-bombing the nostrils. A sort of pungent sickly smell came from the carcass. It was a man. He had been dead for some time. Diamond Jim mused over the situation. The murder had been meant for him. He believed it totally. This was his summer house in Monterey where Jim took his mistress. He had told his staff on Monday that he would be visiting at the weekend. The whole place had been rolled over. Jim hadn't the time to adjust to the scene. Patrolman McLinley, notebook in hand, had an 'I told you so' expression on his face. He was cynical in the extreme. He wasn't one of Jim's policemen so there was no common ground. But the dictum of 'He who lives by the sword will die by the sword', was in his every action. Jim ignored him. He knew Pedro – the corpse – slightly. Usually, Jim preferred not to know his gang in case he had to waste someone. Pedro had fallen from the top floor and lay spread-eagled. It wasn't a pleasant sight.

'Were you here, Sir?'

'Nope.'

'Where were you over the weekend?'

'I was with my wife and family.' Jim didn't tell the patrolman that he received an anonymous call to say that he needed to stay at home. He'd handle that the way the brethren always did. Between brothers.

'You acquainted with your employee, sir?'

'Yep.'

'Was this meant for you, sir?'

'No comment.'

McLinley smiled grimly. He knew the code, and as an honest cop it frightened him deep inside. This would increase a sort of gangland jamboree of killing that made the force and criminal fraternity trigger happy and scary.

'You can go, sir. Stay on the premises. We may need you later.'

'OK.'

Jim was tired. He was tired of the life and the eventual death that was inevitable. He thought of Louis and Levi and the others. He wouldn't tell them. Still, was it Hopkins? Or was it the Greenwich Village mob? Jim felt he could sleep for a week. But he couldn't afford to. He needed to get it right. HH was not someone to take lightly. He picked up his mobile and he rang Martinez.

'Marty, bring up the car. I'm going home.' He knew Martinez was loyal and true. Precious few were these days. He looked at the body and religiously closed the eyes, made the sign of the cross then left. Martinez arrived within the hour. Jim dozed in the car. There was a TV set and drinks cabinet. Martinez kept his distance. He knew his boss.

'Will you be needing me tonight, sir?'

'Nah, enjoy yourself I'll see you in the morning.' Jim trouped into the detached house, surrounded in greenery. Louise looked up.

'Not like you to come in the middle of the day, honey.'

'Nope, it ain't. Can you leave me for a while? I need to do some thinking.'

'OK.' She breezed out. She was cheerful and happy in her little world. Life was refreshingly uncomplicated for Louise.

'Levi will be in for supper. It'll be nice for us to be together,' she said, almost to herself.

'Yeah, yeah.'

He was sophisticated in his outlook. He needed to think. On the face of it, HH could have done it to warn him. It was the sort of thing HH would do but who could explain the removal of the previous stone? No, it wasn't HH. Somebody wanted that stone and wanted it badly. Whoever killed Pedro was looking for something else. He notified Pedro's widow and he'd arrange for their kid to go to private school, which was more than poor Pedro could have done had he lived. She seemed nonplussed when he told her the news.

'The only way – legend has it – you can harm those from Atlantis is to blind them. They have amazing eyes – X-ray eyes that are at one with their hearts. Strike those and you're there. They shrivel up and die. OK, class dismissed. Don't forget the essay I want on Monday, class!'

The clatter of books on the desks and the movement of thirty students rattled through the lecture room. Claudia Klinski wiped the blackboard dry. She was a slim woman of thirty-something years who had an earring in her nose. She was very chic and she wore a scarf round her neck to hide her arteries. She wore corduroy slacks and a man's waistcoat.

The principal looked into her office.

'Can I see you for a minute, Claudia?'

'Yes sir.'

They walked together over the green. The students weren't allowed to walk on the grass. They prattled about the happenings and events of the day. When they were in Judge Petrie's office, he closed the door and took his phone off the hook. It seemed unusual to Claudia but she waited for him to settle.

'Two men from Washington want to see you. Here's their phone number.' He handed over the number. 'Now you know as much about it as I do. They say you're an expert on antediluvian history and they want to pick your brain. Basically, that's it.'

Claudia put her hands in her pockets absentmindedly. The Principal dismissed her. 'OK, that's all, Claudia. Mind you ring them.'

'OK, sir.' Claudia looked seriously at the Principal. Then she left and walked purposefully across the campus and reached her office. She dialled.

'McMillan.'

'I believe you wanted to speak to me? I'm Claudia Klinski.'

'Oh yes, Miss Klinski. We'll send a car to collect you straight away. It'll be at your home address within the hour.'

'Thank you. How long will I be?'

'Could be the weekend, Miss Klinski. Pack an overnight bag, please. If you ever need anything, my name's McMillan, you can get me on Wilmington 3984. Night or day. OK?'

'Got it. Wilmington 3984. Yes. See you soon.'

'Yes, Ma'am.'

Claudia Klinski sat down. She was beat. She had worked hard

all week and she didn't know what this was all about. Still, she'd soon know. She lit a Lucky Strike. The tar creamed her very innards. She rarely smoked. Perhaps when she drank. But she always kept a packet for emergencies. It tasted lousy, but it was a lousy day. She'd finished with Rob and she felt lonely. Now she was completely on her own. She'd been going out with Rob Cronin for over a year and basically she knew it was going nowhere. They were good in the sack but they fought like cat and dog outside it. It had cost her a promotion, Claudia felt. Well, it was history now. She blew her nose.

She retraced her steps and put on a neat mini-skirt, grey and piped with white lines. She selected an open cream blouse and put on her New Age bracelet, which she'd got last Christmas when she and Helen had gone mad shopping. When she'd showered she relaxed for forty minutes. The car came about within the hour. A suited chauffeur greeted her with casual charm and she fell into the luxurious leather seats. They cruised through the outskirts of New York and Claudia took in the skyline. The chauffeur kept his distance – she was grateful for that.

'We've got you here to brief us on the legendary city of Atlantis, Miss Klinski.' She listened as the large, genial man named Wainwright greeted her.

'If you need anything, don't hesitate to ask. You are the guest of the Defence Department.' The words rippled off his tongue like an ack-ack gun. He was polished, good-looking (and knew it) and superficially warm.

Well, I'd like some steak and a massage, Claudia thought but said nothing.

'This is Colonel Jeffries and I'm Rob Wainwright. We liaise between the Defence Department and the military,' Wainwright finished. 'Here's your badge.' He gave her a clip-on visitor badge with her name on it. She put it on.

'We'll have dinner at eight sharp and begin at 9 a.m. tomorrow morning. Anything else. The time is yours if you'd like to go to a Broadway show. See Lentil here,' and he pointed to the chauffeur who blinded her with his ivory teeth. She nodded.

'*Sunset Boulevard?*' she said.

'Give me ten minutes', Lentil hollered.

She sat through *Sunset Boulevard*, aware that she was on her own. At the interval she helped herself to two dry Martinis so she felt not so alone after the break. Then, taken home in style, she fell into bed.

'Damn, damn, damn!' Claudia howled. 'The curse. Today of all days it had to come.' She had brought one tampon and an extra pair of knickers and rued her luck. She was a feisty woman with attitude at the best of times but now she'd eat 'em alive. The mature men usually loved her. It was the youngsters that rattled her cage. Still, she'd go on.

'The show must go on,' Claudia said to herself outside in the lift as she descended to the room she had been requisitioned to. Soon they arrived there and she found she was a guest speaker in front of a group of ten men. All different ages and stages. She'd boned up on Atlantis with the books she'd brought and she felt, PMT apart, that she was in mighty fine fettle.

Wainwright stood up. He was wearing a chequered bow tie with a pale suit. *How much of it is for me?* Claudia mused.

'Gentlemen, you are the *crème de la crème* of the defence force. You've earned your spurs. But nothing is going to prepare you for what you're gonna hear this morning. Remember that you are bound by the Official Secrets Act at all times. Good luck to you. It's my privilege to introduce to you, Miss Claudia Klinski of New Camp David University. She is an expert on what you are about to hear. So without further ado I'll pass you over to her. Don't treat her as a piece of skirt. Give her your attention and your respect.'

You could hear a pin drop. All eyes were on Claudia. They were either overawed or waiting to see her fall on her tight little ass. Either way it didn't matter to Claudia.

'Gentlemen, I feel like shit because it's the wrong time of the month so please bear with me if I sound snappy.'

Applause of a genuine velocity ensued and Claudia realised that they were all immediately on her side. She held up her hands in mock humour. They shut up like a bunch of nuns.

'OK, who'd like to tell me about Atlantis?'

A short, stocky guy of 5'8" stood up and put his hand up. Claudia motioned to him to start.

'There is supposed to be a lost city of people who disappeared under the sea when the wrong age in the earth came around.'

'Precisely, sir, thank you. None of us really know when Atlantis was formed but there is supposed to have been a war on earth in 3000 BC when the dark powers of magicians and sorcerers tried to assume power. Rumour has it that three hundred humanoids built a deep sea craft and disappeared underneath the seabed. Imbued with air tanks from their empire the blue boys, as they called themselves, used primitive suction techniques to create a huge bubble on the seabed. It was a mile high by a mile square and they took with them sacred stones to create the buildings. The magicians and sorcerers were content to rule the earth; they went underground as the heat in the earth billowed. So there were two societies. One underground on the seabed in an immense bubble and another ten miles beneath the ground bearing the purveyors of magic. For a thousand years – to 2000 BC – the people on the seabed grew tails and became mermaids and mermen. No tangible proof is on record with the exception of the antediluvian maid found in 1998 AD when some Japanese divers were trawling for a sunken ship. The immense-ness of the find was akin to Carter's discovery of Tutankhamen's tomb in 1922. We are still dredging up whatever knowledge we can over the maid. We purchased the maid from the Japanese and at the present time we know this – the girl, she was about twenty-two, had a fish tail with scales and had very sculptured breasts. She wore ruby earrings but what was amazing was that her eyes were topaz in colour and seemed to be very precious stones. The Defence Department has put a top secret priority on this find, so only I, and Professor Kopanski at Berkeley University in Califor-nia are privy to the details. Her blood, I can assure you, appeared to be blue – it was caked inside her. She hadn't been dead for more than a week. Her hair was blonde – real blonde – and she was 4'11" tall. She had been using a tool to dredge excrement at the rear side of her tail. This we opened after some time. Her fin was fish-like. It was very powerful. Steps are being taken to embalm the antediluvian maid and discussions at Defence Secretary level are going on as to how she is to be kept.

'So, from 2000 BC the city seemed to be thriving. The mermaids and mermen were able to breathe underwater. They quarried the surrounding area from which the city was built with precious stones – not unlike to the New Heaven and New Earth that is talked about in the book of Revelation in the Bible. Some theologians believe that Atlantis is exactly that. In 1500 BC Gregory the Wise repelled a supernatural rebellion from the young guns who wanted to seize power and take over the city. Gregory died in its defence and has been canonised in Atlantean history. Thereafter there was a rule that evil should not pervade Atlantean society and the city went under the custody of thirteen warrior priestesses who are trained in the art of psychic and martial warfare. Ninety-five per cent of Atlanteans are peace-loving individuals and they have a king and queen who are both full of psychic power and enlightenment which is for superseding our psychic power. They have had no industrial revolution and some say that because of the peace, they live to be 300 years old.

'Their diet is that of raw fish and octopi, and their liquid refreshment is a sort of wine called 'pepe' that does not intoxicate them. In fact it gives them hallucinatory dreams and visions, which makes them wise.

'Rumour has it that Atlantis is centuries ahead of us in terms of medicine, science and education. They are gentle, kind and fun-loving in a peaceful way. They are said to spy on our world and it has been said that UFOs and such like could be evidence of their sorties. This has yet to be proved. Because it is dark under the sea they use a sort of gold metal that shines with a sort of luminosity. A stone with these attributes is rumoured to have been found recently, though no-one knows where it is at present. Their eyes had ethereal power and it is rumoured that they are the equivalent of our heart. Therefore the only way to kill them is through their eyes, which can see in the dark with the skill of a cat and more. They are said to be superhuman because of their ethics and they are immune to viruses such as ours. They possess healing devices that make our advances on HIV-positive cures look like whore's twitch.' Applause. 'That is all gentlemen. Any questions?'

Genuine applause ensued and Claudia drank some orange juice hungrily. She had obviously been a hit with the men and she smiled in mock-abandon. She found them full of genuine respect and admiration for her knowledge. She smiled at Wainwright.

Benny viewed his pad. There were pictures of Jimmy Hendrix – a manic experience, and Bob Dylan – sub-conscious protagonist of virgin truth. This place had been Benny's home for the last two months during the spring of 1970.

He remembered how he'd confronted his mother when he'd stolen his case-notes from the files office. How he'd discovered that he had the same prognosis as his father, without any aiding or abetting. He had hurled abuse at his mother. His rage was frightening, even to himself. He remembered how she told him of her marrying a softly spoken Irish-New Zealander who had a scholarship to Queen's College, Cambridge. And how she had been a physiotherapist at Addenbrookes Hospital just after the war. Bruce McClennen had been suffering from what was then called shell-shock. It was an unknown quantity in those days. They did not know much about it. Elizabeth had taken pity on him and they had married in 1945 after the conclusion of the Second World War.

Then they had Benny, born in 1946 and set out on a Dutch troopship to the romantic setting of New Zealand. The plan was for Bruce to retrain and attain a teaching post in Christchurch. With his qualifications that would not be a real problem. To be English-educated was highly prized, never mind having a scholarship to Queens, Cambridge.

Then it all began to go wrong. Bruce became a different man. He would sit all day in the same position, staring at the walls of the cottage. Hour after hour, day after day. He was no longer the man Elizabeth had married.

Then he would stay out late out all night, which frightened his wife. He was patently spending time with other women and two-timing her. She became alarmed at his bizarre behaviour.

Then it happened. The straw that broke the camel's back. He picked up a cut-throat razor and advanced on Benny's cot announcing manically that he would annihilate the family. He was quite obviously out of his mind. Elizabeth, in true maternal style, picked young Benny up and raced out of the house. She ran all the way to her family doctor who put her up, and under the New Zealand law of the day, was able to file for a divorce. All this was unknown to Benny who had been told that his father had been a strong, silent Gary Cooper-type parent who had died of pneumonia when Benny was six years of age. Benny's rage was insistent. He had arrived at the mental hospital aware that there was the supposition of schizophrenia about his behaviour.

Benny never let the mob know about his instability. He had met Karl in the Criterion, a pub in Upper North Street in Norwich. The pair had taken to one another, warming to each other by telling each other stories, each trying to outdo the other. Benny told Karl of his desire to be a villain. Karl had stored it in his memory. When Massa Charlie told Karl to form a team to retrieve the precious stone from Diamond Jim's home in Monterey, Karl contacted Benny.

'We do not want any trouble, Benny,' Karl had hissed. Benny nodded sagely, with more bravado than he personally felt.

'I will give you the address. We want you to search the place when everyone is absent to find a piece of rock probably in a drawer or locked suitcase.

Benny broke into the Chevrolet. It was a safe car, much used, and its colour – grey – was inconspicuous. Benny linked the ignition wires and fused them together. The car spluttered into action. He noted that there was half a tank of petrol in the fuel gauge. He'd have to rob a garage to fill up. He drove off into the sun; driving slowly so as not to draw attention to himself. He was dressed in dark clothing and he kept a balaclava to use at the garage. Robberies were usually for smack and were two a penny, plus the police were stretched and undermanned.

He pulled the job and it went like a dream. He pushed the Hispanic girl onto the floor and filled up in juice. Another car drove in just as he was leaving. He still wore the balaclava. He'd discovered the balaclava was best from an Irish crook whom he met in England. American crooks tended to wear Ronald Reagan masks and so on, but Benny preferred a balaclava. It gave an impression of insane menace and reduced people to pitiless wrecks. He had told the Hispanic girl not to move for thirty minutes if she didn't want reprisals.

So he was equipped for action and ready to go. He drove to the house without much ado. It was a two hour drive. The Chevy was a joy to drive and it had New Jersey number plates. He'd discard the car on the return journey. Benny told himself that as a self-respecting crook, he was a perfectionist.

So he rounded the back of the house. It was a monied house. These people deserved to be robbed, he told himself. The rich-poor divide chided at his temples. He possessed a kind of contrived hatred inside him in which he was Robin Hood liberating the poverty-stricken masses from oppression. He really believed in his mission.

Benny skirted the side to the back. This house had an immense garden. Somebody loved the outdoors. He selected a small window, having dismantled the alarm system with his own kit. He smashed the window. All was silent. Then his arm opened the inside handle to the window. He felt the thrill of doing something exciting. This was better than sex. It was for him the ultimate high. He felt weak at the knees as he moved cat-like through the study door.

Suddenly he was inside. He had a perverse desire to see the hidden life of his prey. He began in the study, opening and closing doors. He felt his trusty stiletto in his side pocket. He touched it reassuringly. The whole operation took time. But Benny had it. He'd planned to do it in the dark and he carried with him a cheap torch which highlighted what he was looking for. He had strict instructions not to be messy and not to let the inhabitants know what he was looking for.

Benny felt a kind of heady dizziness in his head and he paid no attention to it. He felt groggy but he supposed this to be his reaction to the job.

'Aha! I've found it!' Benny unrolled a largish wrapped object. Unrolled, it was a stone – like a rough piece chipped off some-thing. But at one corner it gleamed like the polished silver glasses of a souped-up Cadillac 'Eldorado'. Benny was intrigued. He pushed it into his bumbag and fingered the stiletto again. Then everything went black.

Claudia was tired. Her 'performance' in front of those men, although successful, had been stressful and she badly needed to sleep.

'Miss Klinski, I am swearing you in to be a consultant for what we are about to do. Needless to say, the ground that we shall be covering will be top secret and offenders will be dealt with seriously if information falls into the wrong hands!' Wainwright accentuated every syllable and vowel and revelled in the authority he spoke with.

Stupid boffin, Claudia thought but meekly said, 'Yes sir.'

'You are given the afternoon off but we will reconvene again at 7.30 p.m. Clear, Miss Klinski?'

'It will be my pleasure, sir,' Claudia smiled secretly. She possessed the ability to be a woman in a man's world. She had had a gentle father and a strong mother and she followed her mother's lead.

That afternoon she went to the top of the Empire State Building. She loved the view. After, in the subway, people got out one by one as they travelled along the line and she found herself alone in her carriage with a Puerto Rican gangland punk.

He went for her immediately. 'Give me your money and I will let you go, Je-ez missee!' Came the inevitable. He stood to his full height. He had on a pair of battle fatigues which were ripped and a lime green vest top. The tattoos – worn to terrorise people and a credit to his macho street cred were a radiant evil.

'Oh no! Don't kill me, please!' Claudia countered. The Puerto Rican relaxed. It was to be his last move.

With cat-like dexterity, Claudia caught hold of the punk's hair. She pulled his head right down as she pulled up her knees in one easy action, smashing them into his head. It hurt. Then, with dastardly bravado she let loose a left-handed uppercut to his face – breaking the punk's already broken nose. He fell over her and as she deftly side-stepped him she muttered cynically, 'Another triumph for feminism, Claudia girl.' She left at the next stop and sweetly caught the next train. She didn't want the police department involved. Not when she was about to do something interesting and adventurous. She patted a hanky over the blood on her tights until she could take them off in her hotel.

'*Que?*' the man said.

Benny felt awful. The man was clothed in a workman's overall; he was probably the gardener and he had been alerted by the light of the torch in the study. Benny thought fast. He had to have anonymity. He couldn't afford for this man to be able to pick him out in an identity parade.

'C-c-can I have a c-c-cigarette please?' He said. The stammer could always be relied upon to come on when he was nervous, which was how he felt now. Benny felt for the stiletto. He fished high and low. Where was it? Oh, jeez, he saw it on the ground about five inches to the gardener's left. The gardener gave Benny a cigarette. Benny inhaled deeply, his head was spinning and the cigarette multiplied his drowsiness. But Benny's desire for survival was strong. He picked up the rock from his bumbag and handed it to the man, whose arms went out to catch it.

Then swift as a King Cobra, Benny coiled onto the floor, swivelling onto his back and raising his knees for protection. He needn't have done it for the gardener recoiled subconsciously. Benny didn't think. He picked up the stiletto in one movement and dug it deep into the man's midriff. They were eyeball-to-eyeball. Benny could smell the garlic on the man's breath. He looked into the eyes of a dead man. He fell to Benny's feet. Benny picked up the stone and ran. He stole another Chevy and drove, high as a kite.

'So this is crime,' Benny muttered to himself. 'Then I'm the king!' He allowed himself a smile, then adjusted the speed to slow to the limit, nodding to a passing police car, aware that they were probably only interested in their next coffee break.

'Don't be stupid,' he muttered. 'That was my first kill. The police, the pigs, they're mugs. Here comes Benny Rogerson – watch out, Bonnie and Clyde!' The car smooched its way along the road through the New Jersey Turnpike and into Queens where the car was jettisoned. Benny was high on his adventure. He had to find Karl. He didn't pause to think that they had wanted a clean job.

He was expendable.

She looked at the lake. It was clear and she could see to the bottom. There was colour in the rocks and stones underneath. She glided along the water's edge, and she felt guided along the pathway. She was holding an object. It was large and in fact she had to purse her fist to cover it. It was covered. As she moved along in the wheelchair she seemed preoccupied with something. Giant goldfish swam along the edge. She was impervious to them. Then she looked at the object in her hand. It glistened and gleamed in the afternoon light. It seemed to be multi-coloured, and it changed colour as she rubbed it. Its light was perhaps the one thing that was the most amazing about it. It seemed to grow in glistening colour as the girl in the wheelchair wheeled herself along the coast of the lake. She came to a stop. Her thoughts were centred on the lake itself. There was a ripple on the water's surface. She stared at the lake, her hand still covering the stone. She stared for a long time. Then a head appeared from the water; it was the head of a giant turtle-like animal. It was, in fact, a terrapin. Its head was displayed boldly.

The girl in the wheelchair fixed her gaze at the terrapin's head. The head exhibited the features of ET but the mouth was sunken inside the muzzle. The eyes were inscrutable and deceptive. The girl put the stone down on her lap and searched for something in her blanket. Then she found a bag and began to pick something out of it. She hurled bread pieces into the lake. First she threw to the left, then she threw to the right, then to the middle; each time, the head surfaced and gobbled the bread. The girl was speaking to the creature. The creature was gesticulating with unfeigned excitement. This went on for thirty minutes. The girl let the bread go down for two to five minutes before she threw out another piece. The whole performance lasted the best part of an hour. The girl and creature seemed to merge into a whole. It was like some mating dance. The spectacle continued until the bag was nearly empty.

Finally the girl threw the last piece of bread straight at the terrapin. As she did she lost her balance. She straightened up in a colossal jerk and her spine wove her upwards. She, like the terrapin, jerked herself upwards. The stone fell from her person into the lake. The wheelchair clattered to the ground, throwing the jewel and the girl into the water. A blanket fell to the side. The wheels of the chair span crazily. The girl was white with fear.

'Help! Help me! Help me!' she was heard to call.

David had changed into his jumpsuit which was a velvet navy blue. He was looking at the reference to Atlantis in his encyclopaedia.

'Rivers of blood! And a pearl of great price will be a key twofold to the secret recess of the city of Atlantis. Beneath the seas the pearl will translate the location of the exit to Utopia.'

The writer here refers to an allegorical tale that was fished out of a cave on the island of Mustique in the West Indies.

The cave was at sea level, and the writing carved in a child-like hand. This was the only source of reference on Atlantis and up until now it had meant nothing.

David mused over the commentary and could not understand the sense of intoxication that he felt as he read the script. His cheeks became red and his nose white. His breathing became exaggerated and he felt both drunk and light-headed. He sat down. He couldn't explain why he felt as he did. He did not tell a living soul of his experience as he would be laughed out of his research scholarship at St Kitts University. Yet he felt a chemical reaction when he heard the word 'Atlantis'. He seemed to be groaning from within. It was like a heady form of drug. David had drunk wine and taken LSD in the sixties. He'd smoked marijuana and he'd taken amphetamines. David had drawn the line at heroin and cocaine. Cocaine was the rich people's drug. And David did not come from the rich part of town. He was the son of a civil servant in the West Indies who had sent him to Eton where David excelled at squash, fives, tennis, cricket, rugby and so on. He had not performed well at academic subjects. So much so that he had had to be sent to a crammer where he sat for three A-Levels which he passed. Once at university, David gave it his all. With the exception of squash, David gave up all games. It wasn't that he couldn't work, merely that he hadn't got his priorities right. With the exception of girls, David grew to like to acquiring knowledge. He became a bit of a boffin, reading till late each night, about five days a week. On weekends David learned about girls. Tall girls, thin girls, fat girls, dark girls, light girls. In fact just about every type of female in the spectrum came under David's scrutiny. He loved them all. And he had the common touch. He permitted himself to be off the leash at weekends. However, girls were not his only interest. He soon became obsessed with folklore and ritual magic. This became a magnificent obsession. David attended groups and clubs, all of which he did out of office hours. His appetite for Camelot, the Grail and Merlin became legendary. So much so that he was permitted to return to the West Indies and study witchcraft and folklore at St Kitts.

He was funded by a mystery benefactor. David felt obligated to whoever was subsidising him and he developed a pagan faith. He developed the ability to worship the 'Mother-Goddess' and 'Horned God' of the old religion. He developed this interest by joining an Alexandrian coven in St Kitts. Or rather, he was recruited.

David had received a phone call at 1 a.m. one morning inviting him to join. He accepted the clandestine invitation and he was initiated into a craft bearing doctors, accountants, policemen and teachers among others. The allegiance was for life. It did not preclude one from following one of the five big religions: Islam, Buddhism, Hinduism, Judaism and Christianity, but each was considered less spiritual than his left hand path. He noticed how his fellowship cast fear into people by the way they put their knives and forks down. Yet David was only a third trained degree initiate. First and second degree were that of fully-fledged Priest or Priestess respectively. David was on the list to move into Inner Sanctum Eldership. He was nearly there but he could not expect to gain his spurs without the help of those more spiritual than him. To attain Inner Sanctum Eldership you had to be forwarded and seconded by those in the Holy council. As David did not, with a few exceptions, know the eleven who were in the council, he could not achieve anything without waiting. He was aware of the procedure so against his best wishes he remained patient, and proud of the place he had reached in the Temple.

He kept to himself his kinship with Atlantis. So he set off through the grounds of the university. He felt drawn to the lakeside without knowing why he was being pulled there. He had run along the side of the lake when he heard the cry for help.

Whoever was in danger had powerful lungs. He increased his speed. As he came closer he saw an upturned wheelchair at the lakeside and a blanket of a turquoise hue. A hundred yards off he heard the cry of a woman.

'When you come close, close your eyes, please.' It had a haunting melody and David complied with the request.

'Push the wheelchair into the lake, please sir.' The 'please sir' was both beseeching and provocative.

David obeyed.

The wheelchair was upright in the lake. She was under the water. She had a turquoise waistcoat on and the look in her eyes was mesmeric. She was like a Madonna with a Pinocchio nose. She was exquisite in every way, except for that nose. David drank in her beauty.

'Stay there, sir. Please turn around.' David did.

'Give me my blanket, sir.' David reached for the blanket and handed it to her. He waited two minutes. He heard her puffing and panting, and he wanted to help but she had requested he face the opposite way. Then she motioned to him.

'Turn me round and pull me out of the lake, kind sir.'

He did so with difficulty. She had hidden whatever bodily deficiency she had underneath the blanket and David thought no more of it.

'The stone, I must find the stone!' she wailed.

'What type of stone?'

'You will know it when you see it,' she replied calmly and her eyes slotted into his. He felt weak with unsuspected passion. But this was a spiritual feeling as well as physical and he felt stronger for locking his eyes into hers.

'I'll look for it,' he said petulantly, considering it to be a female whim.

'Don't doubt it, David,' she called behind him.

He turned in horror. 'How did you know my name?'

'You had it put on your jumpsuit, David Marchbanks,' she cooed. David believed her but he felt enchanted by this strange maiden who was obviously a cripple but whose presence dictated his every whim.

'Believe and you will find the stone, David.' She called him David again, as though she knew him. He began to trust what she was saying. As he did he felt himself pulled slowly but powerfully

55

to his right. Then it became more powerful and he saw beneath the water, a kaleidoscopic and huge stone. He reached for it. It was heavy. He trawled back to where she was on the lakeside.

'Believe and you will receive your utmost desires.' She fixed him with a look that went through him. He shivered. Then she smiled and David became warm.

'Walk with me across the path,' she said.

They walked along the lakeside path. Suddenly David realised she was dry. He asked her how this was.

'It's nothing,' she replied. 'I see you want to learn.' She turned her wheelchair around and fixed her eyes on him again. Slowly she breathed heavily and David felt the warmth he had known concerning Atlantis. Then she spoke.

'Tomorrow your catarrh will be gone forever.'

'Can I see you again?' He wanted to say 'my love' but he dared not.

'If it is meant, we shall see one another again. Just now I need to relax and overcome my condition.' She pointed to her face which was white. David nodded and looked sympathetic.

'Goodbye, my love,' she whispered under her breath and they parted.

Chapter Four

T-Rex ached this morning. He was the world's leading authority on Atlantis. He was himself an author of some renown. He was a playboy writer. But he was different to the other playboys in that he did it all from a wheelchair.

In 1968, T-Rex – real name Tennessee Reilly – made his first pile of money. He had specialised in the swimming pool business for the rich and famous around Beverly Hills. However, his accident had occurred during a violent twister in Texas; he was left paralysed from the waist down. The tornado pirouetted T-Rex through a front door and down some steps, where his spinal nerve was trapped behind the bone. He could move but it was painful.

He liked to surround himself with beautiful people. His valet, One Round, was an ex-Mr Universe. In fact, One Round had actually come second in the contest. The two men were drawn together by their love of the supernatural. One Round became part of T-Rex's team in '71 when his company had gone bust and T-Rex had saved him from dishonour. One Round, faced with his wife Isabelle leaving him, had looked set to take his life. T-Rex joked that he could look after a cripple – himself – and learn the true meaning of humility.

One Round was grateful for the second chance. T-Rex cleared all his debts and this was how he would repay. But he wasn't a servant. More of a friend. Both men were *bon vivants* and at times T-Rex got One Round to tell him of his experiences with the opposite sex. One Round became T-Rex's eyes and ears.

One Round was as intelligent and as devoted as a St Bernard dog. He helped T-Rex in and out of bed and to and from cars. He was always by his side, acting as a minder as well as anything else. Both men would playfully score points off one another and One Round was a trustee of T-Rex's fast-growing fortune. He, T-Rex, went from providing swimming pools to supplying residences to the super-rich. Thus he was in an excellent position to know film stars, singers and presidents.

Nobody knew where T-Rex came from; he kept it a secret. It became a fixation. Many a TV host 'died' trying to pry out the truth from the non-conversant T-Rex. He played the game hard and tough. He was an expert shot and an aggressive gambler. His interests included boating and he had a steam boat moored along the banks of the Mississippi where he played a nightly game of poker. In this game he put up the stakes and offered the opportunities for all prospective gamblers to try their luck against him and One Round.

They would spend many an evening together deliberating which hand to play and arguing with one another as old friends do. One Round was allowed to be rude to T-Rex as no-one else dared. But the rudeness was always in jest. It got so that invitations were addressed to T-Rex and One Round. T-Rex turned down all attempts for people to invite him without his muscular minder. T-Rex was beautifully ugly. He adorned himself with jewels and gold dripped from his person. He also wore red and green suits. Only wearing them once before giving them to charity. He spent thousands on his clothes. One Round always wore one colour – whether it was red or black or white. Together they were the darlings of the social set. T-Rex possessed a dry wit and One Round was the beauty. Many a social event was livelier for their presence.

But T-Rex was rumoured to be ruthless. Rumours of how he did things in his operations were rife. He was reputedly sitting in a lift in one of his buildings once when a motorcyclist lit up in the lift. T-Rex hated smoking.

'How much do you earn?' he enquired.

'Four hundred dollars a week,' came the surprised reply. T-Rex wrote a cheque for the amount and duly gave him his notice whereupon the motorcyclist thanked him very much and walked out to his bike which was labelled 'Perfect Pizzas'. T-Rex had wrongly assumed that the motorcyclist was in his employ. That story passed into the annals of T-Rex history and he liked to tell it against himself, to show that he was able to laugh at himself. He called himself 'the ugliest man in the world', and surrounded himself with beautiful things and pretty girls. However, not everyone knew that T-Rex had appetites of unusual sexual scenarios. Only One Round knew the truth on this matter. T-Rex tended to strike fear into people's hearts. He was skilled at administering pain to people. The Beautiful People set were oblivious to that and with enough cash to buy themselves out of danger, they were rather intrigued by T-Rex's tastes.

One evening T-Rex decided to avail himself of his Mississippi river boat but before he could his mind went back to the girl he had seen on the television, and the mesmeric hold she had on his personage. It had been the *Nat Saturn Show* and she had talked about UFOs. She'd lit up the place. She was a breath of fresh air. He'd been smitten on the fact that like him, she seemed to be crippled. He used the word 'crippled' because he hated the middle-class sympathy that he was given as a wheelchair user. He was adroit with his minder at gaining every possible advantage with his chair and he did his best to look pathetic in order to get his own way. People opened doors for him and made room for him when he purposefully appeared lost and helpless.

T-Rex bought up shares in Kayley's newspaper; he gained 41 per cent of the shares but she was clever – she held 51 per cent of all the shares. She was an astute businesswoman, who played her cards close to her chest. They had finally met at a shareholder's meeting. She'd been introduced to him. T-Rex never usually made himself available to go to such places. He personally had majority shareholdings in over a dozen companies from space travel to chocolates, and his empire was growing. He'd seized the opportunity when, on the television show, she'd plugged the fact that she wanted her show to be owned by the public.

T-Rex was on the phone to his stockbroker that day and he was only able to purloin 41 per cent of the shares. At the shareholder's meeting T-Rex had made sure that she and he met. He turned on all his charm, oozing it from every pore. When he needed to, T-Rex was unstoppable. Men, women, all types, fell at his feet. He was so much larger-than-life, and the world would be a poorer place without people of his character, he believed.

For some reason that T-Rex couldn't understand, she was

impervious to his charm. She seemed to play by different rules to him – to the world in general. She was uniquely her own person. Her eyes, topaz when she was calm, ruby when she got angry, absolutely conquered T-Rex. Somehow she held power through those eyes. When they touched hands, she looked through him and he felt like a little boy at the front of her class. It made him want to possess her even more and he changed to Plan B. He would use a pseudonym and purchase another 16 per cent of shares in the name of H. Barrett. She had obviously sold some of her stake which meant that T-Rex had power over her company now – if not over her. He went to work on her CV. He found out that for the last three years she had been the proprietor of her monthly magazine on the paranormal and UFOs.

But before that time the girl had not existed.

T-Rex put his best agents on the job but they had come up with nothing. This excited T-Rex even more – because she was one of two things. Either she had a secret life with many skeletons in the cupboard or else she played by different rules. Maybe she was like T-Rex; an entrepreneur who had decided to change her past and reinvent. The more mysterious she became, the more T-Rex wanted to find out. Everyone had a price, he reckoned, and he had never been wrong in his fifty or so summers. So what was hers?

T-Rex invited her to dinner on his paddle steamer and she had conceded and accepted his offer, although he felt that she was according him a favour rather than accepting the benefit of his prowess and hospitality.

So they talked and T-Rex realised that she spoke only of the present, never of the past. It was as though she had never existed before the past three years. She'd only discuss her monthly paper which he noted meant a lot to her – or so she led him to believe – but it could have been a bluff on her part. He asked her what she'd do if he foreclosed his shares and effectively destroyed her monthly paper with all the power he held with his declared 41 per cent of the business. She had looked dismayed, though he couldn't be sure because she was a hard one to read, especially possessing those eyes. She had stared into his beady eyes with a passion that he couldn't match and he looked away, none the wiser. When her eyes targeted T-Rex's eyes he found himself getting an erection so he decided it was best to avoid direct eye contact – for now anyway. Until he knew how to handle her and at best, what her price was.

So aroused was he that he attempted to kiss her full on the lips and she had rejected his endeavour vehemently. He grew angry inside, and true to his nature he wanted to destroy what he couldn't possess. He felt his old hatred rise inside him and he saw no need to quell it.

So Kayley became public enemy number one to T-Rex. He had to conquer her even if it meant destroying her. At whatever price it took. T-Rex became very moody and difficult to handle. And true to type, he tended to vent his emotions on One Round who was always the closest to him.

David boarded the river boat. It reminded him of those western movies he'd grown up with as a kid. Its destination was New Orleans and it was going to take a few days at the speed it went, which wasn't fast. David was going to visit his old Professor, Pablo Rodriguez, for a week. Both men were close, especially since David had inherited Pablo's faculty. He had not been given the position of Chair of Paranormal Studies but he was definitely keeping it warm for Pablo. Twenty years separated the two men but they were so close they could have been brothers as far as the outside world could tell. David warmed to the theme of his week's holiday. It was summer, and he'd done all his marking and so the time was all his; he had nothing hanging over him. Besides, a river journey appealed to his sense of adventure. David had heard that there was a professional poker school on board the steamer. In fact it had been part of the reason he'd chose this mode of transport. David fancied his chances at poker and he'd been taught to play semi-professionally by his stepfather. They had spent three days and nights in the Middle East playing each other whilst his mother had plied them with wine. His father had taught him all he knew. And then, when the gloves were off, David had beaten him. So he fancied himself as a poker player. He'd probed the desk clerk about poker school but he'd been told that the cruise had been for purely recreational purposes. But far from putting David off, it had egged him on.

Once aboard David breathed in the river air and enjoyed the peaceful picturesque atmosphere. Daniel, David's cabin steward, acknowledged David's probing to play in the poker school and had said non-committally that he'd 'ask around'. Then one evening a letter appeared under his cabin door, grandiosely inviting him to drinks with the proprietor of the vessel. David smelled success and replied to Daniel with a gleam in his eye. The cabin steward smiled warmly as David pressed a twenty dollar bill into his hand for the favour.

The next night David went to the lounge to meet his host. He was surprised on both accounts to see what he did. First he was introduced to T-Rex in his wheelchair which embarrassed David more than his host, and then he saw her.

The girl from the lakeside.

'Kismet,' David murmured beneath his breath. The girl seemed to be so sure of herself. She was with the owner who had invited him to 'sit in' on the poker school, that evening. They would commence at eight sharp. And there would be no limit on the bets. That would be the only rule.

Chapter Five

He walked in, took in the atmosphere and sauntered casually around the room. It was 7.50 p.m. and he, David, was wearing a sharkskin dinner jacket with a pair of black trousers and a matching black bow tie.

The room was green. There was green baize on the table, which was a large Camelot-type table able to take between eight and sixteen people. The walls were Regency-stripe. The carpet was a Wilton-type twist carpet in a light green hue. David looked up. There was a glass window in the ceiling and there was light in the top. David noted all the facets of the room. He noticed place-settings. He was placed directly opposite T-Rex, next to Nashville David, the high roller, on his right. Nashville, as he was affection-ately known, wore buckskin clothes. Even his shirts were hide. He had made his fortune in cement and he could afford heavy losses. He was known to be a gifted gambler but blackjack was his particular flavour and he was here to make up the numbers. To David's left was Mr Chen, an inscrutable Chinese gentleman said to have two gambling houses in Manila. He wore black with a miniature check shirt and a green bow tie. He was blind and had with him a huge German Shepherd. On Chen's right was a delightfully flashy young woman, Fou Yeung, who was his eyes and ears. She had an ample bosom which Chen used as a tactic when negotiating business deals. She wore a black jacket, a white blouse and pillar-box red mini-skirt. David liked Chen for his courage.

There were only six players that night. To T-Rex's left was Lightnin' Willie, an exceptional card-shark, who was vulnerable when he drank too much. He played colourfully and he and Nashville would probably be ready to lose $50,000 tonight without feeling it. To T-Rex's right was Miss Lucy. She was a mulatto. Built on the heavy side, she'd exposed cheats in poker games before. She wore a Royal Blue flowing robe that came from the shoulder down to the floor. She had been known to carry a knife in her boots. Today she wore high-heels. She was a crony of T-Rex's. Some said they had an on-off relationship although nothing was proven and both participants weren't the blabbing kind. She held shares in T-Rex's property company and, whenever she was around, she stood in a school of poker. For a woman, Miss Lucy was very masculine. The story went round that when the foreman and players of her football club were meeting her for the first time, one of the players said, 'I have a nice view of your boobs from here.'

To which Lucy replied, 'Well, it won't be so good when I sell you to Peterborough!' So she had a tough reputation and she smoked Havana cigars. She was a maverick, who ran her own road; forty miles of bad road.

Then there was T-Rex. He looked resplendent in his coat of many colours, said to be made for him by Gianni Versace before the latter was wasted outside his home in Miami. Rumour had it that T-Rex was evening the odds on behalf of his designer friend. T-Rex wore a dark blue shirt with a Cambridge blue tie. His trousers were Black Watch Tartan – a dark highland tartan which broke all the rules of fashion but worked very well with the multi-coloured coat. On his face T-Rex wore dark green shades with ivory mounts. To T-Rex's shoulder sat in an exquisitely beautiful girl in a wheelchair, whose lips were kissable and whose eyes were emerald green. She wore flamingo red and had a Scot's shawl with a skean dubh brooch attaching it to her left shoulder. As their eyes met, David felt, he thought, strength running into his veins. He was half in love with the girl but he didn't trust her power. It was something he had got to get used to. She looked away and David felt weak within himself and he felt the warm glow of lust inside. He decided to fixate on T-Rex and not the girl – for this evening anyway.

'The game is five-card stud poker. The dealer will deal in two rounds. The deal will go round to the right anti-clockwise, or widdershins if you're into Wicca. The school will finish at midnight sharp; unless you are bankrupt all players will play till that hour. The order of precedence of cards will be as follows: a pair, two pairs, three of a kind, straight, straight flush, full house, straight flush royal, straight flush four of a kind. There will be no cheating. A new unused deck of cards will be used after each hand with a full house or more.' David listened to the master of ceremonies and the referee barking out the orders. He wondered what he would be up against tonight.

A waitress served drinks. There was something about the drinks that David couldn't place properly. They seemed OK enough. They were served in large schooner type glasses. Green in colour, they were exquisitely refilled after every full house. He looked at the glasses. The coloured glass seemed correct to him. He'd have to use plan B.

The cards were dealt at first by T-Rex. To Miss Lucy, one; Mr Chen, four; to David, one; to Nashville Dave, one; to Lightnin' Willie, four. Then four, one, four, four, and one to make up the obligatory five. The first hand was jackpots. Willie opened for $50. Everybody came in for the ride. They took the cards they wanted but everyone knew that Lightnin' had two jacks or more. David drew four new cards keeping his ace as a kicker and folded, getting a pair of threes. He watched the game. David liked to watch. T-Rex was bullying people, but the gamblers, astute to the last, said nothing and did not react to the chiding. Willie opened the bidding for ten. Dave saw him; David was out. Mr Chen saw him and Miss Lucy was out. Willie had exactly what he'd gambled on (a pair of jacks) and he won the hand.

A pair of jacks to start, David mused to himself. He subscribed to the school of counting the cards. In a school of six you'd have six five-card hands on the table before you started to draw. That meant thirty cards were dealt; if everyone drew three cards that came to eighteen more so that was forty-eight cards in a hand. It didn't work out that way. Since there were fifty-two cards in a hand it became possible to see or accurately suspect every card in each person's hand.

'First blood to me,' Willie said. No-one replied. Everyone thought a lot in a school of poker. So Willie was a boaster. He'd study the other players. Nashville looked calm but Dave could see a red glow to his nose. Nashville wasn't here to win, it more as a fun thing. He made an honest buck playing with rich people with money to burn. He was on his second marriage to a Filipino girl and she sat behind him occasionally touching his hand protectively. On declaration it had been agreed that loved ones could play or look on. Miss Lucy had a glamour girl at her side. T-Rex won the first round with a full house and all players lost approximately $100 each. The sherry was passed around and suddenly David saw it. T-Rex's glass was double-bottomed. That meant when he took a drink he had half the amount everyone else had. So T-Rex was outfoxing the gamblers early on, was he? David smiled to himself.

Nashville and Lightnin' were speeding up on their drinking. *T-Rex probably paid them $50,000 to come in on this school*, David thought to himself. Miss Lucy didn't drink. Her voluptuously beautiful partner drank her portion. Mr Chen was a cautious player, he liked to 'see' people but he wasn't a heavy better. You could frighten him out of a hand with an honest bluff.

So it was T-Rex and Miss Lucy. David viewed the cards. T-Rex was about $100,000 up after they had played for two hours. How was he consistently winning? T-Rex had won a lot. Miss Lucy had won about half of his stake and David was down $10,000. He'd brought $100,000 but had only declared $50,000.

The cards fell on the velvet baize again; four to Mr Chen; three to Miss Lucy; one to T-Rex. David dealt methodically. He split the deals to cuts of three or four of a kind. There were three aces in the deck and David was counting; four to T-Rex; two to Lightnin' Willie and three to Nashville Dave. He quickly upped the hands to five per person. One to Chen; two to Miss Lucy; one to T-Rex; three to Lightnin' Willie, and two to Nashville Dave. There were three aces and four jacks in the previous hand and David had intentionally given T-Rex four jacks in one throw. He wanted to know how he'd bet with a good hand.

T-Rex looked like death. The waitress came round with the sherry. *Odd choice, sherry*, David thought. Lightnin', Nashville and Chen kept drinking. T-Rex stoked up and David held on to what sherry he had. Miss Lucy let her popsy drink.

'Up $10,' Miss Lucy called.

'Your ten, and fifty,' T-Rex purred.

'I'm out,' said Lightnin'.

'Me too,' said Nashville.

'Your sixty and twenty,' David smiled at T-Rex.

Miss Lucy packed.

'Up a thousand,' T-Rex smiled.

'See you,' David sighed.

And it was, as he had supposed, a four jack hand. So David *was* counting the cards correctly. He began to slur his words.

'I l-i-k-e you,' he meowed.

T-Rex smiled indulgently. Suddenly the wheelchair girl hissed something in his ear. He turned white, and his tie nearly burst. He stuttered to the next dealer. He didn't look Kayley in the eye.

'Cochon,' he yelped again, his eyes lazily viewed David's shoulder. Then David saw it. Behind David was a small mirror which showed the back of the players. And T-Rex kept peering at David.

So there, my beauty, David thought. *I have you hook, line and sinker.* David made a cool $30,000 on the next nine hands.

Lightnin', Nashville and Miss Lucy packed out of the school so there was only T-Rex, David and Mr Chen. It came to David's deal; up until now David had taken up his hands in ignorance, not knowing that T-Rex could see his cards.

David dealt. There were jacks about, three, he thought, aces and twos. He'd placed the twos in the pack.

Three to Miss Lucy – jacks, David thought, *one to T-Rex, a wild card.* David dealt himself one card – another wild card. Then he took a rare slug of sherry. T-Rex was pleasantly in front of him. He would have to keep sober. Then he dealt the remaining cards. Two to Miss Lucy; four to T-Rex; four to himself. Who would have the jacks, the aces and the twos? David changed his method of play; he sneaked a quick look underneath the five cards. T-Rex looked apprehensive and nervous. He seemed strained. He took some of his own sherry. The wheelchair girl whispered something into T-Rex's ear. Mr Chen put $100 into the pot. T-Rex put in $200, David put in $210. Mr Chen put in $1000. T-Rex put in $1000. David put in $1000 and added $50,000. T-Rex looked at both players. Lightnin' and Nashville and Mr Chen's girlfriend all paid attention.

Mr Chen packed, losing about $1000 but panicking at the height of the deal.

'Nice 'ere, innit?' David purred drunkenly. T-Rex put in $50,000 and added up another $50,000. You could smell the atmosphere in the room. Outside you could hear the din from the blackjack tables and the croupiers barking 'Les jeu sont fait'. David eye-balled T-Rex. T-Rex eye-balled David. This was honour. Who was this puppy who was challenging the champ? A bead of sweat formed on T-Rex's hand. David wiped his face with a handkerchief. He was nervous and drunkenly extrovert. David milked the time and his position.

'You fat, little man. You're bluffing,' he snarled.

T-Rex retorted, 'OK, puppy, show me what you're worth.'

David reached, or rather lurched, to his inside pocket. There was a cheque for $50,000. He reached for it and nonchalantly hurled it in. All eyes were on the table. You could hear a pin drop.

T-Rex said nothing. The girl whispered something in his ear. He snarled, 'Excuse me a second,' and left the room.

The referee froze play. Lightnin' and Nashville talked of the last high-roll. There was a glee in their voices.

Then T-Rex re-entered the room. He took out of his pocket the contracts for Kayley's monthly paper and put in his 55 per cent of the company.

T-Rex was effectively offering David the chance to own the girl's paper.

He was giving him the girl. *What had she said to him to make him to do that?* David wondered.

'Will you excuse me for five minutes, please?' David asked the referee. He was given time. He went out, made a call to his bank manager. What he said remained constant. David re-entered.

'Put the river boat into the pot and I'll vouchsafe $250,000,' David said without a slur in his voice.

T-Rex wrote the IOU for the river boat. So it was the girl and the river boat resting on one hand in the game. Not even Lightnin' Willie or Nashville Dave had seen a game go this high.

David was sweating all over. He reminded himself that he needed a shower, whatever happened. He kept his cards face-down for the first time.

He wrote an IOU for $250,000, courtesy of Coutts. The referee took it and nodded to T-Rex.

'See you, sir,' David spoke.

T-Rex said, 'Three aces.'

David stared impassively into the green baize. The fake drunkenness was unreadable. Then he opened his hand: one two; two twos; three twos. David stopped for effect, then he turned the last card over – it was a two. Four twos beat three aces. The referee spat. T-Rex grimaced. David had made an enemy. The girl smiled into David's eyes. 'Well done,' her eyes seemed to say. They were topaz-coloured.

Chapter Six

'Rumour has it that in the Himalayas there is a race of men who hold the world to ransom.' David digested what the girl was saying. She had no small talk. It was all or nothing with her.

'How do you mean?' he asked, as he looked at her. She was perfect. She sat in her wheelchair overlooking the Peak in Hong Kong. They had booked in at the Mandarin Hotel – it was a lovely holiday – she was very precise and David did not take her for granted. When they had met it was as if they had known each other forever. She had those come-to-bed eyes. Such eyes. Men killed for the likes of those eyes. The eyes alone had a beauty and a language all of their own.

'I do not come from your world, earthling,' she had said. David didn't like being called an earthling but he had no choice. She had absorbed the winning of the company with a phlegmatic purity which puzzled David. Her eyes changed colour and she seemed to be able to read his thoughts. He felt he was getting in too deep. He was embarking on a journey he hadn't been ready for. David was an intelligent non-PC person. Political correctness to David was the result of a few very insecure people being conscious of their position and getting everyone to pay for the consequences. David spoke his mind which made him excellent as an *agent provocateur* but not really the right calibre for out-and-out leadership. A more diplomatic person was needed.

Kayley, as he discovered her name to be, had none of these complications attached to her being. She lived in the now and she was a giver.

'When the time is right, I will show you wonders beyond your kin. I will take you to see my people who will supersede anything you have met before.' David believed her but he didn't quite know what to expect next. Was Kayley for real or was it a bluff? He'd seen enough high-powered psycho-buffoonery to last him a lifetime.

'If you discover the truth about me you will meet a misfortune. But now we must find something that will help us find my people.' She kept speaking in riddles, which on the lips of others it would have been too far-fetched. She spoke with a mock-sarcasm and she had a dry sense of humour which was infectious.

'I live in a wheelchair because I walk badly,' she had said to David. He had let it pass, feeling deep inside himself that she would in her own time reveal all she needed to when she was ready. Now did not seem to be the right time. He held his patience in check. He knew he was being assessed for fidelity. She would look at him for a long time. She possessed an agile brain that translated the human mind with thoughts of the ultimate clarity.

'I talk seriously because I haven't learned to laugh,' she had said enigmatically. David had a thousand and one questions for her but he held them all in check. Had she been a shop girl at some London store, David would have treated her differently. Yet somehow she seemed a unique person indeed. David found himself very much in love with her. But it was a deep-rooted spiritual type of love – not the lustful kind. It was the deeper sort of love and David had not experienced this before. She only called him 'earthling' when she was painfully serious or when she was proving a point. They had gone to Ireland, to Donegal's ancient and unsullied land. They had found Donegal tweed and seen an old-fashioned weaving loom. The Celtic crosses seemed to have significance to Kayley. David grew to love her sensations. She had so many faces. 'The lotus has many faces,' she had mused, while they were touring the Donegal land. They had got to know one another and she trusted him with her wheelchair. In Donegal she showed him something new about herself. An eagle flew down to her and perched on her shoulder. She croaked to the giant bird for ten minutes before saying goodbye by clapping her hands.

'Do you believe in me yet?'

'I believe in you, Kayley.'

'I think you are near to where you need to be!'

'You're in the driving seat,' David mused. She relented and seemed to make a decision.

'When it is midnight come to my room and I will reveal more of the real me.'

She smiled at him and he remained serious because that was what she wanted him to be. He suspected that the wheelchair was a double bluff but he did not know what she wanted. He was possessed by a sort of reverent fear and it was with grave intent that he called on Kayley at midnight.

'Come in.'

He walked in.

He wasn't prepared to meet a mermaid lying in her bath. She met him with a coy shyness which broke the ice. His eyes and mouth were opened wide. He waited to hear what she wanted to tell him.

'I come from the city you earthlings call Atlantis and I need to find the other part of this stone.' She showed him a carefully honed stone which seemed to be shaped like the curve of a bay. The curve seemed like a C-shape and the line went straight to the edge of the stone.

'I possess spiritual power that you people on earth have lost. We are highly sophisticated on both psychic and supernatural levels. We are one with animals in the animal kingdom. We possess the gifts of healing and we are able to see inside people's thoughts. Thus I was able to know what you thought of me when you first met me! We can do this without actually giving away our thoughts.

'We can see into the future when we want to. Thus we can live a long time. We have sophisticated equipment in Atlantis where we can operate on our person and we can 'convert' a normal man or woman into a merman or mermaid. Although once we have 'operated' it cannot be reversed at all. I need to find the brother of this stone to identify where on earth the exact place is to re-enter the city of Atlantis. That is why I need it, David. And we will dance, we will dance with the angels.' It was fitting that Kayley said that. Her eyes looked into David's. They said a million and one things.

There and then, they were lovers in spirit. A mermaid and an earthling shared something special. Something rich, something real. It touched their hearts; then their eyes met and they danced with the devil till midnight. They had no fear, just love. Unmitigated love; a love unfettered by the mores of the day; unbridled by the wings of fearsome fortune, enslaved by dark passions and desires of fleshly lust. Yes, even the angels danced for them, such was their purity – an androgynous union of minds and spirits, entwined in the different unity of their earthly bodies... awake dark love of the night, don't sleep for it is a long, long time before they twitter in evensong. They will light a fire, in which shall perish the thoughts of outrageous minds. Sweet death will unify them in spirit; then cometh the morning after the night of our true desire, when we will dance with the angels and they will play a million sonatas. The lips of mighty seraphs will breathe on a heaven-sent day. It could be the earth's final day for all they care; lips that breathe good fortune and die not with the despising of the flesh. Drink the wine of youth; let them caress the immortal carcass of purity. Sleep well my love, the angel's song will sound with loud symbols of sweet union; sweet bird of youth, forever young and always old. The day before yesterday brings in a solid future with sweet embrace. The moon waxes and wanes and they are loved and lit by moonlight, not gaslight. Sail away on a silver moon, solid gold inside. There is a moon inside them all and a sun of righteousness channelling them forward. They are young, they are vital, such is their love. Sweet angels mimic music at the break of day; so they will love for always and forevermore, till hell freezes over, and as in life, they die a little.

David reached forward with his hand and gently touched her lips. She smiled and her mouth opened in mock laughter. He kissed her. It was their first kiss. It felt rich and pure. It was so natural. They intertwined and David felt through his clothes the coil that was her body. She murmured as they kissed. It wasn't a grunt, more of a shudder. She twisted around and shook her hair in answer to him. Her Bambi come-to-bed eyes spoke to him gently. Their oneness was indeed special. The eyes were so trusting. Like those of a child. They said nothing. Each had their own thoughts and thought of pure things and savoured the moment.

Diamond Jim had had the precious stone cleaned up by De Beers. He was a little perplexed. The attempt on his life had lapsed into history but Jim was prepared for anything. The people nearest to him were scrutinised by his perfectionist's brain. The gem market was prosperous. Jim changed his driver and his minder. He was fastidious about that.

The jewel was splendid. Jim looked at it in his office. It shined like a beacon. It was so bright Jim had to squint. He was deep in thought when his secretary said to him over the phone.

'The gentleman from Sothebys has phoned to confirm that they will auction the gem at 10.00 hours on the fourteenth of this month.' That was two days away. Sothebys were intrigued by its uniqueness and although they knew it to be a rich gem, they had never seen anything like it. He had only to wait.

The Cabinet Minister's secretary had alerted David and Kayley to the sale at Sothebys on the fourteenth of the month. Kayley had to come because she was *au fait* with the twin stone. It belonged to her. David did not like her being implicated but there was nothing he could do. The Foreign Office Intelligence Service were posted details of the sales quarterly and had deduced that the 'unique gem, one of its kind of unknown origin' was their stone. Kayley and David were comfortable in each other's company. Now that David knew that Kayley was a mermaid he felt he was privy to a great secret. He was both excited and confused. It presented a practical obstacle to his pure love. It did not complicate matters but David knew deep down that he and Kayley would need to make a choice at some point. But now they had work to do.

'Lot sixteen is a precious stone of unique value. The only one of its kind known to mankind. Our experts are assured of its preciousness by the gem-like qualities in it. But no one knows where the stone was mined. Perhaps deep in the ocean or high up in the Himalayas. Can we start the bidding at £100,000?' The auctioneer's polished diction droned across the assembled old money, new money and agents acting for the super-rich.

David had a brief for £250,000 from his cabinet overlords. They desired to keep it in the UK, for presentation to the R and A museum.

'I have £110,000 there…' And so the price went up and up. There was an Iranian gentleman keen to have it but he only bid £200,000. David signalled at £205,000. The auctioneer continued.

'I have £205,000 from the gentleman at the front. Going... going... gone, at £205,000.' The hammer fell and the gem was theirs. Kayley and David smiled. If this was it, she would be able to pinpoint Atlantis.

Back in an opulent office in Whitehall they positioned the twin stones next to one another in the bright light of a super-charged angle-poise lamp. Sure enough the halves fitted together. It became whole.

'All we need now is an atlas, to pore over the islands in the world's oceans,' said David. Kayley nodded her assent. They had become easily yoked to each other. Often she and he would think the same thoughts.

They had trouble placing it anywhere on the map until Kayley had an idea. 'Perhaps if we turned it upside down?' she said. They did so and it was soon clear that the place the map showed was the Isla de la Juventad, off Cuba. Communist waters.

'We will supply the deep sea apparatus and boat from Jamaica but if you are discovered we will deny all knowledge of your presence.' The Cabinet Minister's secretary droned.

'Fair enough,' David replied. The race was on.

Chapter Seven

They were diving down in the depths of the ocean. It was three weeks since Kayley had shared her secret with David. He felt honoured. He knew that they were meant to be right for one another but he couldn't get his head around the fact that they were so different. They came from different worlds – literally. David pondered over this in his spare moments. They had spent the three weeks preparing for the dive, accumulating all the deep sea diving equipment, and being briefed by the navy on how to dive expertly. David shielded Kayley from embarrassment by only letting the Cabinet Secretary know that Kayley was going to dive with him. There had been the tense scene in the Secretary's office when Kayley had nailed her colours to the mast by removing the blanket from her knees to show him why she didn't need to practice.

'If this gets out nobody will take me seriously again,' was the first reaction of the Cabinet Secretary. He was astonished and was completely out of his depth, until Kayley turned her powers of psychic wisdom onto him to calm him down. The spiritual power and authority she invoked relaxed him and he became very supportive and obliging. Kayley had used, she told David later, her healing powers. And he had been a good subject. Apart from David, he was the only person on earth to bear witness to the presence of a mermaid. They met daily and were still extremely close. They were like little children sharing a secret. Such was their innocence. It was true, David thought, that at the advent of a new millennium Homo sapiens had lost, through worship of science and technology, that inbuilt intuition and spirituality gifting that had been instinctive in previous centuries.

These thoughts occupied David as they dived. The pair had dived secretly when the boat's owner was not in a position to see that Kayley was a mermaid. She dived exquisitely and, like penguins who were so clumsy on land yet graceful in water, she swam so serenely. She had no need of oxygen, of course. David alone wore the oxygen tanks and snorkel input that was standard navy issue. He had a two hour supply in the tanks on his back. So they descended. He felt the leadership of the operation change hands from him to Kayley. In her presence he felt completely safe. When they reached about five miles in depth they had an incident with a barracuda which swam up menacingly to David. It had been a dicey moment. The large fish loomed, opening its massive jaws. Kayley came between them and began to use a sort of language which David could only guess was understood by the dangerous fish. She put out her hand, free from fear, and stroked the monster. The fish permitted her to do this and, seemingly placated, disappeared into the depths from whence it had come. David could see, through the channel of light his head-torch created, a smile came to Kayley's lips. She seemed amused by David's obvious fear and discomfort.

Slowly they descended deeper. It was very dark down there. Finally after forty-five minutes of diving they seemed to reach the ocean's floor. They had measured their position together with the ship's navigator. They had come out on a naval destroyer and Kayley had stayed in her wheelchair throughout all the briefing and preparations. No one except the Cabinet Secretary and David knew she was amphibious.

They spent ten minutes swimming along the ocean's bottom and Kayley seemed to be looking for something. She seemed to be getting her bearings. They continued to swim along the seabed until Kayley motioned to David to ascend. She seemed to know instinctively that David's oxygen supply would run out if they stayed submerged any longer. So they swam comfortably to the surface. When they broke water David upended his face mask and light and looked long into her eyes. Today they were trusting and confident. It seemed to David that topaz was the relaxed colour of her eyes. And today, sure enough, they were topaz. They shone like lighthouse beams in the fog of an Atlantic rockery. Kayley stayed in the water. She seemed not to want to get back on the boat. David exchanged his empty oxygen tanks for new ones and told the owner of the boat of their progress. Kayley viewed the interaction with a detached good humour. David knew she was excited and anxious to dive again. Something in her manner told him she wanted to leave his world for hers. It seemed like the pull of home – of the ocean – something she had been born to that was occupying her mind.

David complied with her urgency. He intimated with his right hand a gesture for them to dive yet again and her eyes turned to a ruby colour. *Perhaps they changed colour with her emotions*, David thought. Then they submerged again.

This time Kayley led them further to the west of the boat. She seemed sure, to him, that she was taking the right route. David felt a little child's excitement deep within himself that he hadn't felt for decades. He felt like a five year old exploring with his pals.

They swam in tandem. Kayley leading the way; her tail pushed up and down very powerfully and on her front, she wore a bikini top for decency. She didn't seem to feel the cold when she was in the ocean's depths. Even through David's rubber suit, he felt the iciness of the water. His ears felt the pressure as they swam lower. Suddenly when they reached the bottom of the ocean, Kayley became excited. She swooped on a cluster of rocks. Seeming to recognise them, she pointed to a flat surface at the top of the cluster. Holding David's eyes, Kayley motioned to a piece of rock that jutted out of the flat surface. David followed her motions. Then with her left hand, she began to take hold of the six inch piece of rock on the top of the base. Slowly, she turned it clockwise ninety degrees. It moved easily. As she did this, the rock surface slid into the main mass. It was about four feet by two feet. David realised that here was the opening. Kayley gave David a thumbs up sign and he nodded back to her. She dived through the hole.

David followed, his heart all of a flutter with a combination of fear and excitement. About three hundred feet beneath the rock entrance, they saw a whole city. *If people could see this*, David thought to himself in wonder.

The buildings were not huge. They were about a hundred to two hundred feet high. They were of many different colours. There were black buildings, red buildings, green buildings – buildings of all colours. The whole scene looked exactly like an immense sophisticated city or like London or New York. The surfaces of the buildings seemed to be mirrored, so that the whole city seemed to gleam in the centre of the oceanic cavern. It must have been half a mile long by nearly a mile wide.

David swam dumbstruck. So this was Kayley' s home. She smiled knowingly to David who blew her an awkward kiss. She blew one back. David was overawed by the occasion. He was aware that he was the first human to witness the legendary city of Atlantis. So it was all true, he mused. For a few minutes Kayley allowed David to take in his surroundings. The deep-sea sky-scrapers varied in height from fifty feet to two hundred feet and they were about a hundred feet above the highest. As his eyes took in the situation David could see people swimming around the buildings. Like Kayley, they all possessed fish tails and swam along with the greatest of ease. They were occupied with their business. But they wore no clothing. The women's breasts were unadorned and the mermen didn't seem to possess body hair. They were smooth-skinned. They seemed to be unaware of their nakedness. Kayley motioned for David to swim with her down to the floor level. The city floor shone with a sort of gleaming gold. So the buildings were a mirrored blue, green, red, orange, black and yellow and the city floor was a gleaming and shiny gold.

Kayley motioned for David to take off his breathing apparatus, which he did. He found that there was air in this immense hole where the city sat. It seemed to be in a sort of vacuum. He also realised that not only was there air but that he could speak. Kayley broke the silence.

'This is my home. I belong here, David.'

'I believe you, my love,' he replied. She smiled and swam through the air and kissed him full on the lips. David had never loved her more than he did at that moment. He was in a giant world of make-believe. He wished he had a camera.

'Come and meet my parents,' she whispered to David.

'Lead me to them,' he assented.

They swam down to the gold coloured streets, which were even more sensational the closer a person got to them. Their shine was blazingly powerful.

'Your eyes are more powerful than mine. These colours are dazzling my eyes, Kayley,' David said.

'Fear not, my love,' she murmured. And with a forefinger she touched the top of both his left and right eyes.

Suddenly he felt an amazingly powerful and poignant source of energy and power touch his eyes. And they synchronised the colours so that they didn't half blind him.

'Our eyes are the most powerful part of us. The only time we become vulnerable is if our eyes are damaged. I suppose you could say that to Atlanteans, our eyes are equivalent to your human hearts. They are our epicentre. I am giving your eyes supernatural power so that you aren't blinded by our light. Light to us, David, is power. As you need food to nourish yourselves, we rely on light. Food, for us, is a pleasure. That is why on earth I was pale and white as a sheet. Down here, I will be pink, which is my natural colour.'

David adjusted his eyes and found that what she had said was true. She had supercharged his eyes and he felt strength.

'How do you have all this power?' he asked her.

'It has been inherited through many generations. But if you start to believe like a child, you can generate such power yourself down here. But not on the earth's surface!' Kayley explained. David was numbed and had to pause to take in the sight he was witnessing. All the mermaids and mermen were seemingly smiling. It was all so different. They all seemed to be so happy.

'We have no wars or quarrels or arguments here. We are a peace-loving people. The last war we had was over three thousand years ago.' Kayley went on. 'That is why we live to be 250 or 300 years old. We have also virtually eliminated viruses and disease. There is, you see, a connection between ethics and disease. If you are good morally, you don't fall ill. We have proved this.'

Then she motioned him to follow her. Slowly and purposefully they swam through the doorway of a building, red in colour.

Chapter Eight

Archimedes Ajax listened to the radio. The year was 2006.

'This is Radio Kinshasa. Here is the news. The ZAS in Zaire are fighting the government's troops for control of the Republic.' The ZAS was the guerrilla troops, crack troops who were dividing the tribal warfare. They had been at war for six years. Each year AWA – Africa wins again. The newsreader announced the details of the Libyan Premier's state visit to Rome. President Adalpi had one of the safest seats in Africa. He had been into back door politics with the Communists and now had an affiliation with China. The Prime Minister of Italy was fawning over his African dignitary.

The newsreader went on, '...next week, the 24th Olympic games will be held in Johannesburg. The host nation has announced a state of military security. The President of the Republic of South Africa welcomes those who come in peace for the Rainbow Olympics.' President Asayndi was the new incumbent of the Republic of South Africa. Rufus Asayndi was a spiritual soldier. Once a freedom fighter in the French Foreign Legion, he had cleaned up his act and for the previous five years he had been the shadow government in RSA. He was in a unique position to tilt the balance of power.

Archimedes sent a fax to Asayndi. 'Citizen Z to President A. All is set for the twenty-fifth of the month. Please return answer in the affirmative that RSA is in a state of readiness.' He sent it off through his male secretary, a bright young man was good on the piano and who was a joker. Archimedes was always fighting the pain in his war wound. He had, on the last day of the guerrilla war in the Congo Zaire in the sixties, lost one eye and he could only see slightly out of his remaining eye. He had been the logical successor to the Mobutu Sese Seko rule in the civil war of the sixties.

Archimedes was unique in that he had out of kindness taken a commission at Sandhurst – a favour granted through the Belgian government's Red Cross work. The young Archimedes had been a renaissance man. He had studied politics, philosophy and economics at St Edmunds Hall in Oxford. He had been granted an Eton education. He had excelled at sports especially long distance running, boxing and rugby. He had been given a Rhodes scholarship and had played as a wing three-quarter in the varsity match two years running. Archimedes took his position of overlord seriously and saw himself as a sort of latter-day Saviour of the African continent.

He contemplated the fax that he would send to the seventeen addresses that he was overlord to: RSA, Zimbabwe, Zambia, Malawi, Tanzania, Mozambique, Botswana, Kenya, Ethiopia, Nigeria, Egypt, Libya, Algeria, Cameroon, Ivory Coast, Ghana and Uganda. The fax went as follows:

> Operation Liberty. Overlord of Operation Liberty affirms the commencement of Operation Liberty on Sunday the 25 July at 1800 hours sharp. Do not forget the African People's Summit on Wednesday 21 July at 0900 hours in Kinshasa. RSVP by Monday 19 July at 2100 hours. Good luck.'

Archimedes knew that he would need to wait. He was not a patient man. He had taken his English education and then shown his hatred of the British Colonial system. His Zaire-based African standard army had struck fear into every one of the white people in Zaire as it then was. There had been the event in 1973 when nineteen Pentecostal missionaries had chosen to die rather than renounce their faith. Ajax had been commander-in-chief of the operation just before the coup to overpower Mebeli's forces. The missionaries had had a quiet dignity which had impressed the young firebrand. But he had not spared the women and children. There were eight children and four adult women. They possessed a universal peace which riled General Ajax to the bone. As the rifles went off, they were facing the guns with hands palmed in prayer with smiles on their faces. The men, women and children had shown a quiet dignity that had overridden the young commander's authority. Some of his men had turned away in reverence to the Christian God. Ajax had personally given the order to shoot. As the people had fallen down dead, the civilized world woke up. Ajax, aided by his tribal allegiances, had caused a revolution ten days later. He had overturned Mebeli's guard and troops. The latter had shown no resistance and the coup was almost bloodless.

So Archimedes Ajax had been in power for twenty-six years. He was the senior statesman in Africa. He had ruled with an iron fist. Any resistance was solved by an African kangaroo court. Witnesses were bribed and the truth was forced out of anyone who objected to Ajax's control. Archimedes was president of the FANC – the Federation of the African National Congress. In the last few years Cameroon, the Ivory Coast, Ghana and Sierra Leone had joined the previous big six: RSA, Zimbabwe, Zambia, Tanzania, Kenya and Ethiopia, the nations that were sounding blocks for the heartbeat of African affairs. Ajax had looked upon it as his baby. He had delusions of grandeur. He had toured other countries within the federation over the years, forging friendships based on the mutual hate of Imperialistic Capitalism. He had been a lackey of Moscow in the Brezhnev and Andropov eras, and was well connected with the People's Republic of China. He had toured China in '92 after Russia gave up the ghost and although he did not possess nuclear weapons, he had Soviet-made fire-power, tanks and ground-to-air missiles which he had done a deal with the Japanese to copy with their ability as engineers. He had run a scheme where Japanese expertise was purchased in Zaire and he held a formidable arsenal of weapons (the existence of which was secret) which he was ready, willing and able to utilise at the slightest provocation.

Whilst France, UK and the USA had been contesting Saddam Hussein's weapons, Ajax had been linking hands with FANC where he had acted as consultant to such countries as Tanzania, Malawi, Zambia and Kenya. He was, in all but name, the senior patriarch in the continent of Africa and the European and American nations had seen the danger too late. He had treaties with Britain and the US which he had flouted whilst eyes were on Hussein. He was now considered as an evil dictator who was too powerful in statesman-like qualities to cross publicly. Clinton and his successor had sent him aid and education and medical supplies, all of which he had learned quickly about, teaching a whole new generation of blacks to utilize their academic resources. It had been a revolution within a revolution. Clinton had needed allies in Africa and Britain had sent Ajax three squadrons of Tornado jets – happy to land the contracts and ready to allow white people to purchase property and run schools and hospitals in Zaire.

Archimedes had fanned the FANC and although Botswana, Angola, Congo, Gabon, Mozambique, Chad and Niger were not really involved practically in the nationalism of the African nationhood, they did not present too much of a problem to Archimedes' security systems within each country. Black Fascism, as the Brits had started to call it, owed much to the African Federation desiring to purify itself of all mulatto and Eurasian influences. Black Fascism was a term coined by Antony Simkins, a devotee of Enoch Powell, who was an MP for Kingston, Surrey in England. Instead of people fearing Russia and China, Britain and America now saw danger in the rise of nationalism in the continent of Africa.

Ajax was a workaholic. He relied on hard work. He slept for five hours a night in HQ where his 'household cavalry' were a hundred strong. He never stayed in the same place more than once. He used a Secret Service whereby money was given to informers who told on those who planned to usurp General Ajax. His Red Brigade, who were modelled on Hitler's Blackshirts, were absolutely ruthless. Archimedes did a lot for Zaire. Roads were built, the railway was modernised with 125 mph trains linking the main cities. Education was good and he had spawned universities policed by Western brains. So in a way, people never really had had it so good as it was under Archimedes Ajax.

On Wednesday 21 July, Archimedes personally met the dignitaries who visited him in Kinshasa.

Zulelli of the RSA sat to his right. He was a svelte young man, a lawyer by profession, who modelled himself on Nelson Mandela. General Egberti of Zimbabwe was a tough ex-mercenary of mixed blood. Ajax hated him but he needed him. He was like a gorilla in appearance and his wide-open lips accentuated this. Rumour had it that he had had plastic surgery on his private parts as well as his lips. President Zebili of Zambia was a middle-of-the-road man. He had unfortunately bled the education and farmers of his country dry. He was hated and people, both black and white, feared his terrorist views. Ajax trusted him no further than he could see him. But Zebili was Africa. Modern Africa and Ajax couldn't argue. Doctor Sveiluga of Malawi relied on Ajax and had proved a good ally when Ajax was setting up his federation. As had President Tzombi of Mozambique, Doctor Parnassak of Tanzania and General Belitte of Botswana. These three had been founder members of the all-powerful Federation of African National Congress. President Odinga of Kenya, Doctor Ossec of Ethiopia, General Nkomo of Nigeria, President Aswad of Egypt, Colonel Adolpho of Libya, Lieutenant-Colonel Le Mesurier of Algeria, Doctor Gabiddon of Cameroon – all were junior statesmen. They had each one worked as freedom-fighters in the corrupt governments of the moment and with the aid of Ajax's secret police and security services, had overthrown the governments of the time. Bloody coups had ensued. But Archimedes Ajax was whiter than white where this was concerned. And his aid in military crack troops, although America and Britain suspected them of aggravating civil war, was generally unproven.

Suddenly Ajax was the Lion of Africa and he had a very long mane. He had teeth and his bite was deadly. The President of the Ivory Coast. Julias Bende, President Swahillo of Ghana and Reverend Artemis Uko of Uganda were all on the Ajax payroll. The Western countries, suffering by proxy from the dire recession in European and America, were unable to suspect collaboration between the African Congress members. Ajax had encouraged schools, hospitals and universities, aided by the US, in his satellite African states such as Zambia, Zimbabwe, RSA, Malawi and Tanzania. He had become a glorious benevolent dictator to them and his people loved him. Those who didn't never lived to tell the tale. Because there was a treaty with the US, who did not see Black fascism rising until the FANC was seventeen members strong. The Secret Seventeen, as the presidential initiates called them, were powerful together, but weak apart. Much of their nationals were simple, unlearned folk who couldn't see the wood for the trees. The Giant that was Africa was very much awake and General Archimedes was its architect!

'Welcome, gentlemen,' Archimedes boomed. 'I hope your quarters for tonight are comfortable.' An armed guard stood behind each head of state and, emblazoning the outfits of the latter, were Sam Brown belts in colours of the nation concerned. This was for protection against plots. Ajax was paranoid about everything; two people drank his drinks and tasted his food before him. His Red Brigade were bully boys with weapons. He had been shot at and bombed. But Archimedes was a survivor. His word was being listened to. 'You will realise that Operation Liberty will commence at 1800 hours on Sunday 25th July, the exact time of the 24th Olympiad's opening ceremony. Each nation will attack as follows. President Zulelli, you will invade Namibia. General Egberti, your troops will invade Katanga. President Zebili, you will overrun Angola. President Tzombi of Mozambique, Doctor Parnassek of Tanzania and General Belitte of Botswana, you will combine to invade Western Africa, the Central African Republic, Chad and Niger. President Odinga of Kenya, Doctor Ossec of Ethiopia and General Nkomo of Nigeria, you will conquer Somalia, Burkina Faso, Liberia, Sierra Leone, Guinea and Mali. Lieutenant Colonel Le Mesurier of Algeria, and Doctor Gabiddon of Cameroon, you will take over Morocco and Tunisia. President Banda of the Ivory Coast and President Swahillo of Ghana, you will quell Senegal, Guinea, Mauretania, and Western Sahara. Reverend Uko of Uganda, you will overrun the Sudan. You all have secret police who will activate your freedom fighters inside each country. We have dealt with the liaison and the coups during our training sessions. So you will all have a code word for 'action' and you will commandeer army headquarters and presidential palaces.

'There is an information pack for your chiefs of staff to your right. You have been on army exercises for three months now. Those whose enemies are overland will be flown in by *Hercules* with tanks and ground-to-air missiles to arrive at 1800 hours African time. Now, my chiefs of staff will liaise with your chiefs of staff so that we spend today and tomorrow planning the operation with military precision. The briefing will finish with a federation meeting at 1200 hours on Thursday, 22 July, where heads of state and military personnel will all meet in the Great

Hall in Kasabubu Avenue, Kinshasa. We have briefed the world outside that we are meeting to deliberate famine survival, education of our common peoples, hospital plans and scientific progress on our agricultural lands and minerals. We are planning to show the world that nationalism can bring peace to Africa. That is the point of this Summit as far as the world is concerned. On Thursday at 1100 hours I will read a statement regarding our endeavours to a battalion of journalists. Apart from you and your generals, no one knows of our intentions. Armies are on standby for what they understand to be exercise duty and we have armed them to the teeth.

'We will overrun Africa, gentlemen. Good luck and good hunting.' Archimedes liked the colonial swagger with which he was power-drunk.

'Are there any questions?' There followed the inevitable practical issues which Archimedes navigated with his usual endeavour, relying heavily on his aides to pinpoint the root of the problems and resolve them. Ajax was a true psychopath; he hid his killing and madness well under the evangelical zeal of humanitarianism. Might was right to Ajax. Events to come would usher in his greatest hour.

'We will drink a toast to the Lion of Africa.'

'To the Lion of Africa!' was the reply. They all drank in reverence. At last he sat down. Exhausted by his efforts and deeply happy in his grandiose passions as overall Supremo and Commander-in-Chief, Africa was his for the taking.

'*Viva* Ajax! A new age has begun. The age of Aquarius has truly begun. Long live the Lion of Africa!'

Ajax slept well that night. His Red Brigade were stealthily ever present at headquarters. They were posted on round-the-clock surveillance. They never slept. They were the eyes and ears of the revolution.

'Long live the Lion of Africa', was their mood of the moment.

Chapter Nine

Kayley led the way. She was excited. It had been three whole years since she had come to her home city. The beautifully mirrored walls of the buildings reflected myriad colours. Around the edge of the city was a sheet of armour-plated glass. It reached about a thousand feet up into the oceans. Although it was difficult to see with the naked eye you could just about discern the sea water and the tropical fluorescent fishes swimming over the glass dome. Kayley pointed upwards at this for David so that he too could enjoy the poignancy of the homecoming. He looked up with her and marvelled.

Kayley was home.

The tropical fish swimming above the glass dome were akin to birds flying across the sky up on earth. They were small and they darted about the intense blue of the waters above. Kayley felt her heart beat with excitement. She felt as she always did when she returned home: like a little girl once again. Then she moved towards the centre of the city of Atlantis. The roads were simply highways of water, and Kayley surged through them, indulging herself in the pure water. David swam awkwardly at her side. Slowly she led him along the sea lane (as they were called in Atlantis) towards an imposing dark-blue shiny building. This took them about a quarter of an hour because Kayley allowed for David's slower movements.

Finally they reached the entrance. Kayley pulled a lever at the side of the door. It opened, sliding upwards. The ceiling seemed high and distant. Kayley swam gently in with David in her wake. There was a merman just beyond at the doorway. As he saw Kayley he smiled broadly and they embraced one another, kissing on the cheeks. He looked at David with a mixture of amusement and detached curiosity. His eyes queried David's legs.

Kayley said, 'This is my very good friend David, Spero. He comes from earth where you know I have been living and observing these last three years.' Spero nodded and offered his hand in a flowing gesture, bowing as he did so. He did not speak.

'Is my father well?' Kayley asked. Now Spero spoke for the first time. His voice was deep and resonant; throaty and velvet.

'Yes. He is tired, princess, but he is still in comparative good health as you will soon see for yourself.'

'My father had trouble with his heart some years ago. He is the Presiding Minister of our Quorum – you'd call it parliament or congress. He worked too hard and his heart gave out. However, our expertise in medicine saved his life and now, although he still advises the new Presiding Minister, Ka – prime minister or president in your world – he only works on a consultancy basis. The doctors here saved his life and gave him a new heart which will allow him to live out his given lifespan of about 250 to 300 years.' David nodded and squeezed Kayley's hand, knowing how important Kayley's father was to her. She responded by brushing dust from his underwater suit. They were beckoned in by Spero who swam along with them in convoy. When they reached the next doorway, Spero pulled a lever again and the door opened upwards so they could swim into the next room.

This room was even grander. Two mermen sat upon chairs. Kayley waved to the grey-haired, bearded mermen who called out merriments to her in tones like Spero's.

'We have been expecting you, princess. It was time for you to return to us here to report what information you have of the world on earth. We got your message a few weeks ago.'

Kayley swam up to her father through the brilliantly blue water. He held her in his arms and in a long, lingering embrace.

'Welcome to Atlantis, my friend,' Kayley's father said to David, who was taking in his surroundings.

David smiled shyly and replied, 'Thank you, Sir.' The two people smiled – a universal currency among any species.

The other merman turned to Kayley's father and said, 'I will see you tomorrow, Porthos, when we will go over the details of my quorum speech.' Kayley's father, Porthos, smiled his assent and the other, younger merman, swam off towards the door that they had entered by.

'That is the new Presiding Minister whom I have been advising,' Porthos explained.

So Kayley's a princess in Atlantis, David thought to himself. As if reading his thoughts Porthos explained to David.

'My family are royalty in Atlantis and Kayley is our eldest child. Normally I would rule here for my lifetime but I have annexed eldership to Kayley's cousin, Aramis, who is of comparatively young age – a mere stripling of eighty-two. So leadership has remained in the family. My health only allows me to spend some of my time as an adviser to our new presiding minister. Come, have some refreshments with us.' Porthos clapped his hands together and nodded to Spero who swam to a small side door. He disappeared for a few minutes whilst father and daughter conversed in a dialect totally foreign to David. Just as David was beginning to feel left out of things, Porthos addressed him.

'Forgive our rudeness in speaking in our native tongue. We haven't seen one another for three years.' He seemed to speak in perfect English and David was amazed. Again, as if reading his mind, Porthos said, 'We are taught how to speak earth English at school from an early age.'

'Are you telepathic? Twice you've answered my questions without my speaking them out loud,' said David.

'Yes, we are,' Porthos replied. 'You see, we possess gifts you earthlings have long since lost now that you let science and technology rule your culture. You lost that innate spirituality that comes naturally to those who choose to pursue a simpler path. You will find that all Atlanteans possess supernatural powers. We are schooled in it from birth. Have you not noticed this in Kayley?'

'Yes, I have,' said David. 'And I have been very impressed by her gift of healing and by her telepathy. But I did not know that everyone here had the gifts.'

'Yes, they do, my son. We encourage it from an early age in our schools and especially in our homes. Kayley could sense things even before she could talk.'

Kayley turned to David and smiled shyly and playfully at him in that coy way of hers. He drank in her innocent simplicity. It was something that he had lost a long time ago, growing up on earth. Spero then entered pulling a sort of trolley which carried food and drink. Porthos resumed.

'Earth food – especially for you both.' David nodded in a perplexed way, not wanting to offend his august host. Spero served them attentively.

'You love my daughter, my son.' It was a statement, not a question. 'So tell me about yourself.'

'Don't you know, sir?' asked David.

'Yes, my son, I possess the gift of reading minds. It comes in handy when you are in politics, don't you think?' David began to warm to the older man's droll sense of humour and self-deprecation.

David, with Kayley's hand in his, told Porthos about himself in a relaxed sort of way. The old man silently listened and nodded in assent now and again. Then he said, 'And you are an earth policeman?'

'Yes, I work part-time in the British Police Force and also Her Majesty's intelligence service,' said David.

'I know, my son,' said the old man sagely.

'Surely there is no need for me to tell you about myself as you know it all telepathically,' muttered David apologetically.

'But I like to hear it from your mouth, David. As a man speaks, so his heart is. I like to listen to your heart, my son, the heart is very important in our Atlantean culture.'

'Our heart reveals all about ourselves. And it is out of our heart that these sacred gifts come,' Kayley confirmed to David. Then she turned back to her father.

'And how is mother, father?'

'She is well, as always.'

'Where is she?'

'Spero will fetch her,' Porthos fondly replied. He waved them both to chairs and they sat, Kayley letting her tail trace sway in the pure water. Then the door at the side opened and in swam an exquisitely classical mermaid. Like her husband, Leila had grey hair but hers was so long it reached over her breasts. Her face was slim and angular. Her features were slightly hawk-like – her nose and eyes protruded like a golden eagle. Whilst her husband was genial and affable, Leila was aristocratic and full of haughty presence. She was the sort of person all eyes turned to when she first entered a room. David was smitten by her beauty immediately. *This is what Kayley will be like when she gets older,* he thought.

Porthos exuded gentleness and sensitivity. His features were wide and cosy and he looked older than his wife. Leila's grey hair was the only part of her that made her look her age. The rest of her looked timeless. Her features were strong and vibrant. Kayley swam into her long thin arms. They kissed each other's cheeks and held each other for a long time saying nothing. When at last they parted the older woman said,

'So you are the young man in my daughter's heart. For an earthling you're definitely attractive. *And* you love her!' David did not know what to do. She smiled warmly at him.

'Welcome to our family,' she purred. 'May you learn much from your stay here.'

'Thank you, Ma'am,' David stuttered. Then Leila offered him her hand, which he kissed meekly, aware of her age and spiritual perception.

He must have seemed ill at ease for she said warmly to him, 'Fear not, young man, we are a people of peace here in Atlantis. We have been thus for hundreds of years. That is why we possess spiritual gifts which you lack. You earthlings have lost such things through war. We Atlanteans wish you no harm.' With that, Leila swam to a seat and perched on it next to her husband.

'Welcome to you both,' beamed Porthos. 'I am overjoyed to see you. We have so much to share with each other. Let us savour the moments we have with one another. It is a most special homecoming for us. For our only daughter and her loved one.' David felt a child-like innocence he had lost long ago, returning to his soul. He felt he could really be at home in Atlantis.

Chapter Ten

'We face a great trouble,' Porthos said. Kayley and David were facing the old man. Leila was in another room preparing a meal for them to eat. 'We have powers of evil in our midst here in Atlantis, threatening to overthrow our kingdom of peace.'

'How is this so, father?' Kayley asked.

'They call themselves the desert warriors,' Porthos replied.

'Who are the desert warriors, father?'

'We do not really know much about them except that they rule our sewers and strike from inside them. We think that they live deep in the ocean rock face. That they have a stronghold there. They appear to be warrior mermaids and mermen who are committed to overthrowing our kingdom of peace. For thousands of years Atlantis has been ruled by peace and these people seem dedicated to destroying the stability of our kingdom, my children,' Porthos mused.

'Tell us more, father.'

'Only last week there was an attack on the presiding minister. He was shot at with earthlings' rifles. These weapons are not available here in Atlantis so we can only assume that the desert warriors have contacts up on earth. That is why we sent Kayley on a mission – to locate the origins of their distribution,' Porthos carried on.

'I found that their supplies led me to the Cosa Nostra,' said Kayley. 'I was on a mission because these desert warriors, three years ago, were starting to make their presence felt down here in Atlantis. We captured a mermaid desert warrior who told us when asked that her weapons came from earth.' Porthos nodded sadly to David whose mouth was agape with incredulity.

'So that was why you were on earth, Kayley? You never told me the reason when you disclosed your mermaid's identity to me,' David said curtly.

'She wasn't totally sure that you were trustworthy,' Porthos continued.

'Tell us of the attempt to kill the Presiding Minister,' Kayley asked her father.

'It was last week whilst the Presiding Minister was travelling to a quorum meeting with the elders that two desert warrior gunmen shot at him from about a hundred yards. They hit him in the arm. So they weren't very good shots. Still, we were sufficiently frightened to declare a state of alert, which is still in operation. We are scared that some of the people in our city will defect to the desert warrior side. That is why we are really concerned. It is the old conflict between good and evil. We have ruled Atlantis for years by peaceful means. This is the reason why our city is light years ahead of your progress on earth. We have powers to read minds, to heal and to foretell the future. These powers were once present upon the earth before warfare and evil reared their ugly heads and destroyed your supernatural powers!' The very subject under discussion seemed to tire Porthos and Kayley and David asked what they could do to help.

'We can rebuff the attacks down here. But you could help by finding and arresting the people on earth who are arming the spiritual warriors who are terrorising Atlantis from its sewers,' the old man replied.

'Tell us how we can help,' Kayley said.

It was 9 p.m. on Sunday the 25th of July. Three hours had passed since the Olympiad's opening ceremony had begun. Archimedes Ajax was standing by his personal hotline. He had instructed his fellow warriors to report at 2100 hours how the outright assault on the African continent was going. He had five lines open and four aides were positioned on four hot lines. Archimedes had watched the opening ceremony for an hour on television. After that a news flash interrupted the Johannesburg broadcast. A newsreader told of the bloody fighting in Namibia between guerrilla fighters and the country's defence militia. The ceremony had gone off the air as a state of emergency was declared in South Africa. A news team was keeping a morose eye on the bitter fighting that was going on in Windhoek in Namibia. The newscasters looked more severe as reports of fatalities amongst the country's unsuspecting troops came in. Then, at 8 p.m.

another newsflash was made declaring that hard and bitter fighting had broken out in Botswana, Angola, Congo, Gabon, Mozambique, Chad and Niger all seemingly at 1800 hours. Archimedes was drunk with the pleasure of having masterminded the complete assault of the non-FANC countries of Africa. However, he was still tense about the situation. He had given the personnel his five hotlines and he was waiting to hear first-hand reports from his side of the military fence. He knew that the generals and presidents, being at the centre of each struggle, would present him with much more accurate and on-the-spot information than the television network.

It was 9.05 p.m. when the first telephone rang. It belonged to Archimedes. 'Ajax here,' he barked down the line.

'President Zulelli here, chief. We have secured control of the palace guard, the military headquarters and the policy colony. We have actualized severe casualties but Namibia is ours. I have placed armed guards at all places and I am instructing the RSA to bring in more troops that were placed on stand-by in case we face a counter-coup in the coming hours. This is the military position, chief. Any more news yet?'

'Thank you, Zulelli, my brother, for the report. Yours is the first notification we have got so I cannot put you more fully in the picture except that RSA television is reporting on the overall fighting throughout the continent. Continue to be on alert and post armed guards on your captives in case an escape is planned somehow. When you've done that ring me on the regular line to report the position further. Now we need to clear the line to allow the others to report directly to me. Over and out!' He put the phone down aggressively and looked at the rest of the room as he did so. Three of the four telephonists were talking away on their respective phones. Archimedes wanted to be at the centre of everything. He was angry with impatience for news and details. One telephonist put his receiver down and walked quietly over to Ajax's.

'General Egberti of Zimbabwe has secured command of Katanga. He has sustained 20 per cent casualties but Lubumbashi and Likasi are entirely under military law. It looks as if Katanga is ours, chief.'

'Good,' Ajax snarled. 'Carry on at your telephone. There may be other calls wanting to reach your hotline.'

Another phone rang and another telephonist called out to Ajax from his office desk.

'President Tzombi, Dr Parnassek and General Belitte have encountered heavy fighting but they are overrunning the Central African Republic, Chad and Niger. It seems that the military in all three countries were totally unprepared for any invasion and the fighting, although fierce at first, was over by 1945 hours. Niger put up more resistance than the rest, Chief.'

Ajax nodded his approval as he took up his own phone again.

'President Odinga of Kenya here, chief of staff. Dr Ossec of Ethiopia and General Nkomo of Nigeria and I have invaded Somalia, Burkina Faso, Liberia, Sierra Leone, Guinea and Mali. We activated six different liberation forces, all of which have taken over the military, the police forces and security armaments in each country. Fighting ceased at 2005 hours. We are not sure of fatalities but the enemy air forces were massacred due to the use of our ground-to-air missiles and our tanks surround the perimeter of each major city as planned, sir.'

'What about your auxiliary forces, Odinga?' Ajax enquired.

'We are moving these in. My generals are on the job in each country as we rehearsed, so effectively, as far as our invasion is concerned, all serious fighting is over. There are a few frontier skirmishes on Sierra Leone's borders, but nothing to get excited about. We will destroy all resistance mercilessly as you ordered, sir.'

'Good boy,' Archimedes allowed himself to say. 'Now get off the line and contact us at HQ through the other telephone lines as directed.' Another telephonist shouted to Ajax.

'Lieutenant-Colonel Le Mesurier of Algeria and Dr Gabiddon of Cameroon are occupying Morocco and Tunisia. Fighting is still going on and they have sustained 10 per cent casualties but by all accounts it is all over bar the shouting, chief.'

Ajax nodded and gave the man a glare which sent him scurrying back to his telephone. Another telephonist called out to Archimedes.

'President Banda of the Ivory Coast and President Swahillo of

Ghana are meeting with token resistance in Senegal and Guinea after having taken over Mauritania and the Western Sahara. Heavy fighting and bloodshed is going on as we speak, chief.'

'Call President Zulelli of the RSA and request him to deploy his standby force to assist messrs Banda and Swahillo in Guinea and Senegal as opposed to using them to invade and inhabit Namibia. Do it immediately!'

'Yes, sir. Will do,' came the frightened man's reply. Ajax struck fear into his cohorts; his reputation for ruthlessness overrode any type of disobedience in his staff. The blood was pumping manically in Archimedes' veins. His huge face was charged with passion as he spoke.

Another telephonist with more confidence called over to him. 'Reverend Ako reports total success in his conquest of Sudan. He talks of inflicting 85 per cent fatalities on the opposition, chief. A massacre, he said.'

'Good news, laddie.' Ajax smiled. He could relax now, though he wanted to go outside and shout, 'Yes, we've done it!' Instead, he steadied himself and merely played with his Sam Brown military belt. Archimedes Ajax had dressed himself for this special occasion. He cut a fine figure of black African aggression as he towered over the desks in the room. His men seemed excited along with him as they relayed the news to him from each hotline. The clock struck 8.30 p.m. and Ajax ordered the men to cover his personal phone for a moment.

He went outside into the night air. He heard the crickets singing as he paced, deliriously happily, up and down the pathway to his personal headquarters in Kinshasa. The sky was midnight blue and the stars smiled down on him.

'Yes! Ye-e-s!' He muttered to himself and the heavens. He felt as if he could murder a bottle of scotch but he curbed his desire. He had to be in command of his faculties for all eventualities. 'Perhaps one shot wouldn't harm me!' he grinned cheekily to himself as he walked back into his HQ.

This room contained twenty-one manned phones. As arranged by the chiefs of staff, these were the phones that each strike force leader would contact Kinshasa HQ on as they worked out what was what in the individual invasions and occupations. *A hundred and one questions would be answered here*, thought Archimedes as he gulped down a small shot of scotch from the personal bar in the room's sideboard unit.

Christ, that was good. He permitted himself a smile of victory at last. He was, he decided, truly the Lion of Africa now. He would go down in history as one of the great unifiers of African kingdoms. His smile became a grin as he pandered to his megalomaniac thoughts. 'Keep me informed of all events as and when they happen,' he directed the staff manning the phones. 'I am retiring to my quarters for a cat nap. Wake me if it is necessary,' he barked. Then he turned in and threw himself on his spartan bunk in utter exhaustion. Like Churchill, Archimedes Ajax knew how important rest was, especially when in the middle of an important campaign. He slept as soon as his head hit the pillow.

The telephones continued to ring incessantly.

Chapter Eleven

Kayley swam with David at a speed that he could manage. They reached an alcove with space for them to sit. They both relaxed in one another's presence. It had been the first time that they had been truly alone in Atlantis.

'Why were you sent up to the world that I know as earth, Kayley?' David stammered at last.

'We have been monitoring the earthlings' way of life for some time,' she explained. 'And as you've been told I was sent to find out where the desert warriors got their weapons from and to report back with my findings to the quorum here in Atlantis.'

'So the monthly newspaper was a cover that allowed you to probe for the sources of these enemies?'

'Yes, my love. I had to have a bogus identity that was beyond suspicion. The Presiding Council hit upon the idea of my owning and running a monthly magazine on the paranormal and UFOs. It was relatively easy to subsidise me with finances as we merely copied your earth money on our machinery. I started with three million United States dollars. Because Atlanteans have visited the earth regularly, I was able to be briefed on how to run an earthling business. This was four years ago. I was briefed by Kara, my cousin. She has been in the USA as I had, using a wheelchair and charging up her natural batteries by lying in water overnight. We have a lot of technological wizardry which is light years ahead of yours.'

'How did you find out where the weapons were coming from?'

'Kara had a contact whom she cultivated, a man called Diamond Jim Sullivan, who has a reputable front as an international gemmologist. She pumped him for information, having used her telepathic powers with other humans. It took her eighteen months of surveillance before she actually met this man, "Diamond Jim Sullivan", in New York.'

'But how is the mob aware of Atlantis? And why are they providing firepower for the subterranean desert warriors?'

'The desert warriors are not all mermaids or mermen as we Atlanteans are. They are using human form to penetrate earth. You see, we Atlanteans can use our superior medical knowledge to change people from mermaids to human form. As far as we know, a few of the desert warriors have had the operation to become human beings. We have a waiting list for this in our hospital and our surveillance has shown us that three people at least have disappeared after they were operated on. We have not known where until we discovered from our security sources that the desert warriors have been on the earth's surface. The type of laser surgery we do is very new and a more sophisticated form of your sex change operation. The people we have done this surgery on have gone on to earth and are giving us information on the state of earth's affairs. We have people in Africa, Great Britain, the United States and Europe. We think that three of our spies, as you call them, have changed sides and joined the desert warriors.'

David was silent for a few minutes. He suddenly thought of the prospect of his becoming a merman, supposing the Atlantean doctors were to agree to operate on him. He was preoccupied with these thoughts and he didn't really know what he felt about the situation. Kayley knew what he was thinking and took his hand in hers. She leaned over and kissed him full on the lips. Her lips tasted salty and warm and David returned the kiss self-consciously. They fell into each other's arms; their embrace became very passionate. David felt himself getting an erection and tried to control himself but could not. He caressed Kayley's back and shoulders and slid his hands over her soft and gentle skin. She kissed his neck and nibbled at his ears playfully. Then she kissed him full on the lips again, entering his mouth with her tongue and tantalisingly played with his mouth. David turned away for a moment.

'It's all right, my love. Do not be embarrassed about being excited by our body presence.'

'I'm sorry, Kayley…'

She touched his lips with her finger and smiled playfully at him. His face broke into a smile too.

'I know you are thinking of becoming like me. Do not worry, David, it will keep. Let us just enjoy each other and the love we have for each other. My parents really like you. They told me so.'

'I feel so out of my depth,' David murmured.

'If it is meant to be, it will happen. Right now there are things we have to do to help Atlantis.'

'What?'

'We have to return to earth to stop the desert warrior spies getting hold of more earth weapons that can kill. The Presiding Minister was lucky. But the bullets only just missed his person. One of his aides was killed.'

'Your father didn't tell us *that*,' David shot back at her anxiously.

'He doesn't want to upset you or reveal too much of our Atlantean conflict until he knows you will help Atlantis.'

'I see.' David relaxed over this. 'How can we ease the situation, Kayley?'

'We have to stop the desert warrior human beings from receiving more weapons from the mob.'

'How?'

'Kara will help us. She will brief us about this man, Diamond Jim Sullivan. After that it is up to us. I'm afraid we shall have to kill whoever it is for the sake of our people.'

'No, I will do that. I don't want you to lose your spiritual power by doing evil things. I'm a trained policeman. Let me handle that. I can do the killing if it has to be done.'

Kayley rested in his arms, cradling her head on his shoulders and slowly she began to cry. David heard the sound of her weeping. He looked into her face as she sat up awkwardly.

'It will be alright, darling. We must be strong for the sake of Atlantis. Be brave, please,' he pleaded.

'Yes, you are right, my love,' Kayley replied. 'Come, let us go back to my parents. I know my father wants to talk to us.' David nodded. So they swam back to the blue fluorescent building that was Porthos and Leila's residence. Deep in thought, they did not speak as they swam. They only changed course to avoid the other mermaids and mermen swimming in the opposite direction.

Through the seaways a hundred yards from the resonant blue

building of Porthos and Leila, was a small red building. It was a hundred feet high and sixty feet wide. It wasn't as ostentatious or opulent as theirs but nonetheless it was pretty. The red was a blood shade. It was the home of Jewel, a member of the quorum. There were six elders in the quorum of Atlantis: three were on the governing side and three were in opposition. The Presiding Minister held the governing vote in a split decision of votes. Jewel had been an elder for eighteen years. For the last six years he had nursed a resentment because he had been passed over twice for the post of Presiding Minister of Atlantis: once a few months ago to the young puppy, Ka, and before, eighteen years previously, when Porthos had gained a majority himself. Jewel was highly ambitious and he felt he had been passed over unjustifiably on these two occasions.

In the main room of his Atlantean home, eight mermaids and four mermen. They were seated in dark chairs arrayed around the large room. Jewel spoke. He was very striking. His hair was blond and his beard so long that it rested on his magnificent chest. It was also blond. He was muscular in physique and his fish tail was stocky and powerful.

'I have called you here together to talk about our plot to kill the Presiding Minister, Ka. We all know that the mission failed and that Ka's aide was killed instead. This was mismanagement of the AK-47 rifles we have acquired from earth's surface. We have three and we need to be able to use them properly.' He paused for effect. His audience was captivated by the way he vaunted his ambition and lust for power. They, unlike him, were just getting used to traits of evil rather than good and they were very new to it. To be full of greed, lust and ego did not sit comfortably on their shoulders and it showed.

'Zak travelled through the sewers, as discussed, until he reached Ka's residence. He entered the house and he should have killed Ka. But he clumsily missed and has disgraced our movement.' Zak was one of the three mermen, who, under Jewel's guidance, as elder in charge of health, had had an operation to change him into a human being four years ago. Zak, Jay and Zadok were his desert warriors. They had all gone to the earth's surface where Zak had acquired the Russian ex-military rifles from the Cosa Nostra in New York City. Zak had been given the honour of assassinating Ka in which he had failed miserably. Zak, Jay and Zadok sat on a *chaise longue*-type piece of furniture behind Jewel and shuffled uncomfortably at their leader's words. Zak blushed and glared as he listened. He wanted the sea to swallow him up. His two colleagues were no comfort. Jewel's word was law. They had disgraced the movement by this incompetence.

For safety reasons, the three human beings lived in a cavern beneath the sewers in the centre of the rock on which Atlantis was situated. It was ten feet wide by eight feet high and three feet long. They stayed *protem* to avoid suspicion since their disappearance. They slept in sleeping bags on the floor. The three had been trained by the mob's foot soldiers to use the AK-47s but obviously they hadn't been trained well enough or Ka would be dead and unrest in Atlantis would have been established.

'I will send Zak, Jay and Zadok back to earth to talk with our earthling neighbours about more weapons and munitions. If we are to rule Atlantis we will need firepower to protect us and to keep the population of Atlantis under our control and dominance.' As Jewel spoke, he hypnotised his audience. He still possessed the spiritual power that had got him elected to the quorum; he held them in the palm of his hand. They all listened with bated breath. Jewel had gone on a mission to earth before he joined the quorum. He had made contact with the New York mafia all those years ago, and it was by his own hand-written introduction that the three had gained access to America's criminal fraternity. Jewel still used his Atlantis bred spiritual power. It took on a deadly hue of evil which possessed him lock, stock and barrel. He was an accomplished orator and the mermaids and mermen were under his thumb. He had personally recruited each one and this meeting of secrecy was one of many he had convened for the purpose of ousting Ka and placing on his own shoulders the power to control Atlantis.

Jewel's metamorphosis from good to evil had been a gradual one. And he had spent the last six years selecting subjects in Atlantis who possessed the qualities of ambition, greed, ego and the desire for personal advancement at the expense of all others. Each mermaid and merman had been seduced by his sweet words of enticement. He had hand-groomed them and only when he was sure of their complete compliance and loyalty had he introduced each one to the others. This had been for Jewel a lifetime's work and he had no intention of failing, having come so far. He spoke to them for half an hour about his plans for the future and the part they would play in it with him. Every eye in the room was upon him.

As he spoke they became as greedy and ambitious as he and he knew that once the balance of power was broken by Ka's demise, he and his twelve disciples could rule Atlantis as a police state, together with the sophisticated earth weapons that killed, exploded and destroyed at whim. Jewel was impatient for such a moment and he couldn't conceal his lust for power very well. Being a statesman and a diplomat, he was able to disguise his naked greed with an entreatment of persuasive works and enchanting arguments. His audience were putty in his hands and he knew it. Finally he said, 'We will put this behind us. We all know that we are chosen to rule Atlantis and to herald a new age where we can expand and use the earth knowledge from the surface to attain our goal. Each of you I have hand-picked, so do not fail me, my children. We will disperse now until I call you all together again for a new meeting. Remember – might is right, and trust no mermaid or merman except yourselves.' He clapped his hands loudly and immediately the twelve dispersed like good children. Jewel turned to Zak, Jay and Zadok behind him.

'Stay here. I want to explore our future plan of attack. We cannot let one foolhardy act unsettle our followers.' The three humans nodded in agreement.

'What do you want us to do, Jewel?' Zak asked.

'I want you to return to the surface for me,' he replied, quick as a flash, and he began to speak to them differently as trusted personnel privy to his grand design of things. Their eyes turned to bright red, ablaze with pure greed and ambition. Jewel wished he had more than these three for his exploits and to see his crusade as an adventure in its own right. *But these three*, he thought, *are human beings in spirit as well as body. They are only too ready to do daring deeds and take risks for me. I wish the twelve others were like them.* With that, he finished telling them his plans and the three returned to their cavern next to the city's sewers where they talked of their next move amongst themselves.

Chapter Twelve

Porthos, Kayley, David and Kara sat in the main lounge of their blue fluorescent home. Leila was providing the drinks for them. Porthos was 250 years old yet he looked about fifty in earth years. His features were chiselled, with a strong jawline, expressive eyes and a fine mane of hair. His daughter, Kayley, sat to his left. Her eyes were on her father. She gazed at him intently. She had a well shaped face; a little full perhaps, with very puckered kissable lips and her cheeks had a light pink colouring. Her eyes – like her father's – were powerfully expressive; large and Bambi-like. Her hair was dark brown and curled right down to her waist. Today it was curled over her protected breasts, covered tastefully in a natural coloured bikini top. She was pensive and aware of the seriousness of the situation. David sat next to her on a chair to her left. He was dark haired and tall. He cut a powerful figure, his chest swelling with each breath. He seemed, of all of them, to be the only one who appeared relaxed. It was just so for David the more he spent time with these people from Atlantis. He liked their directness and their desire to see good at all times. They had almost extinguished evil in their city and David believed in this people who possessed such perception, insight and telepathic gifting. Next to David sat Kara, Kayley's cousin, who had spent time on earth apprehending the link between the desert warriors and Diamond Jim Sullivan in New York City. She was short and almost mannish. She possessed short, curly blonde hair with a long boyish face that took in everything it looked at. Kara was serious too, waiting for the small talk to finish.

Leila brought in the refreshments. She served everyone and then Speros served her as she sat down. He then left them alone to the matters of the day.

It was 1000 hours earth time. Porthos had called them all together to speak to them seriously. Everyone sensed the poignancy of the meeting. Everyone let Porthos direct proceedings.

'How do you like Atlantis, David?' The old man enquired.

'I love the people and the spiritual gifts the Atlanteans possess. I envy the ability of your people to see good in everything; and I respect your healing and telepathic abilities.'

'Good. Good, my boy,' Porthos seemed preoccupied by other things. He seemed to be waiting for his moment. He hesitated and an awkward silence ensued. The rest of the room was silent, awaiting his lead. He was, after all, the consultant to the presiding elder and a member of the well-respected quorum that ruled Atlantis and had done for centuries.

'Ka and I have been discussing the situation last night and we have both decided that the best move is to put you all in the picture,' he finally said, seeming slightly awkward and still beating around the bush. 'Our surveillance has shown us a worrying development which I need to discuss with you all.' His eyes veered between dark brown and black, the colour of deep gravitas and severity. Kayley's eyes were also very dark, and Kara's were a dark hue of brown. Only Leila possessed green eyes. David looked at each person in turn and never ceased to be astonished by the fluid way their eyes changed colour in expressing their moods or feelings. *Much like mood rings*, he thought to himself, as Porthos seemed to be grappling to find the appropriate words.

'There is evil afoot,' Porthos finally spoke it out. It was obvious that he found it difficult to broach the subject with any real conviction. He was so pure, so good. Totally uncontaminated by the evil of earths people. This was why he had lived so long and how he possessed the gift of telepathy that he'd displayed to David on their first meeting. And how he, like Kayley, possessed the gift of healing.

'There are three desert warriors who are returning to earth to get weapons and munitions to help them make a *coup d'etat* down here in Atlantis.' He paused as if for effect and looked at everyone in turn. Then he took three photographs and handed them around. They were pictures of Zak, Jay and Zadok, the mermen turned human beings. Porthos continued.

'Our medical hospital has pictures of these men after they did operations on them four years ago. They have disappeared but we know that they have been on earth and in touch with earth's criminal fraternity. They have collected your Russian AK-47 machine guns and we believe that they possess more than the one they used to try to assassinate Ka with a short while ago.' Kayley looked at the pictures. Zak was ruggedly handsome with a cruel smile, and a scar on the side of his chin. He was clean shaven.

'He is the ringleader,' Porthos told his daughter curtly. 'His name is Zak and he is fearless. It was he who shot at Ka. It was a miracle that he missed and hit Ka's deputy.'

Kayley looked at the next photo. It was of a man with a wider face with a sort of snarl on his cruel lips. His eyes were cold and calculating and he was bald. She passed the photos to David once she'd looked at them.

'The second man is Jay.' Porthos told her. Then she looked at the third picture. The face was young, handsome even. Almost menacing.

'The third man is Zadok. He is a psychopath. He showed these tendencies before we operated on him. He is the most dangerous of the three. We hoped the operation would have a peaceful effect on him but we were wrong.'

'What do we need to do?' Kayley asked her father who appeared to ignore her in his effort to carry on the conversation.

'They are led by a man called Jewel who is part of our quorum. He sits in opposition to us. He has spent time hatching a plot against all that is decent and good in Atlantis. We have been watching him but he is cunning and we have no proof that he gave the order for the attempt on Ka's life. We also do not know how many mermaids and mermen he has on his side, or what he plans to do next.'

Kayley looked knowingly at David. She knew what he was thinking through her telepathy. David was used to her powers by now. He smiled gently at her.

'All we know is that they are going to earth, if they have not done so already, to obtain AK-47s, revolvers and grenades. We know that they have done business before with a man in the New York mob called Diamond Jim Sullivan and a man called Frankie Hayes, his trusty lieutenant. It was Sullivan who sold the one part of the Atlantis gem at Sotheby's which you bought for £20,000 of earth money.'

Kayley nodded to her father, remembering the auction and how she'd got the jewel for less than she had expected. Porthos seemed to be deep in thought as if there was a conflict within him between good and evil. Finally he spoke out loud to David and Kayley.

'I want you both to go up to earth and offer the two stones to Diamond Jim free of charge.'

'Go on,' David said.

'On the open market the two gems – as a set – would fetch £1,000,000 of your earth money. This is what I want you both to do. I want you to give these priceless gems to Sullivan on condition that he agrees not to provide Zak, Jay and Zadok with the munitions our sources say they are looking for.'

There was a long pause when everyone was deep in thought and nobody said anything. Then David spoke in a measured tone.

'Kayley and I will go up back to New York City to prevent these hooligans from getting the weapons. I am a trained policeman and I would count it an honour to defend Atlantis from such a fate.'

'Thank you, David, I knew we could count on your support. Our sources say that the three men are after twelve AK-47s, twenty-four Colt .45 revolvers and fifty grenades. Our sources are reliable so there is much at stake which I don't need to reiterate to you all. We cannot let Atlantis fall into the hands of evil minds and lose the peace that we have enjoyed for thousands of years from the rule of Julius the First onwards. Your mission is an important one, dear ones.' Kayley went over to her father and delicately kissed him on the cheek and then embraced him gently.

'Even if I lose my supernatural powers I will do everything in my power to foil these raiders, father. David and I will start immediately. We have no time to lose.' She nodded grimly at David who nodded in agreement.

That afternoon, David, in his wetsuit, diving tanks and face mask, and Kayley with her fishtail were swimming upwards through the ocean depths towards the light of the sky. David felt alive for the first time in quite a while. As he broke water he felt free and at home again. He pushed up his mask and viewed the vast stretch of water that is the Caribbean Sea. Kayley looked to the Isla de la Juventad off Cuba and slowly they swam to the shore of the latter. It seemed like light years that they had been away but in fact it was only a week or so. David was in his element back on earth and he took the lead. The rich cane fields were precious to David and he looked at the peasants using their machetes to cut the sugar cane. *Castro's Cuba has not changed*, he thought. Then he put his mind to the job in hand. He got a blanket and carried Kayley inside it for cover. They flew by chartered helicopter from Havana up to Miami where David got a wheelchair for Kayley. From Miami they flew to Kennedy airport, and so with Kayley ensconced in her blanket and wheelchair, they alighted at the Trump Tower Hotel in Manhattan. They were both tired and they took two rooms on the sixth floor with adjoining doors. That night Kayley and David slept in the comfort of excellent suites. Kayley got up at midnight and spent the night snoozing in her bath. David enjoyed the comfort of a luxurious bed. He was dead to the world.

'Come to Gold Arts Jewellers on Broadway at 2.15,' Diamond Jim had said to Kayley when she reminded him that she possessed the matching half of the priceless jewel he had sold at Sothebys for £20,000 a short while ago. They alighted from their suites in Trump Tower Hotel having both had breakfast in bed. They descended in the elevator to the ground floor. It was buzzing with opulent guests and celebrities. David took no notice as he pushed Kayley along in her wheelchair. The marble stairs and ornate gold decorations were the last things on their minds. They were thinking only of whether Diamond Jim would accept their proposition and whether they would reach him before the desert warriors did. David was tense and so was Kayley, albeit in a different way. They were both deep in thought. They did not speak to each other. Were they in time? Would Sullivan agree to their proposition? Had the three warriors beaten them to it? As they left Trump Tower, David felt a weakness in his stomach akin to butterflies when he was about to bat at cricket. Kayley did not tell him but she could instinctively feel David's apprehension. She read his thoughts. There was a pensive look on her face. Her eyes were emerald green today. Together they rode in the yellow taxi cab as it sped through the teeming streets of New York.

Finally they got there. David paid the driver. He wheeled Kayley to the jeweller's entrance. 'Gold Arts' was emblazoned in gold on a dark green facade. In the window there were expensive rings, bracelets and chains of all types and sizes. They looked in the window for a short time, pensively aware of the task ahead of them.

'A ruby engagement ring would be nice, dear heart,' Kayley murmured absentmindedly.

'Let's save Atlantis first, darling,' David smiled back at her. They went in slowly through the door.

A beautiful oriental girl in a grey suit stood at the counter before them. Inside there were watches, chains, bracelets and rings. She looked curiously at the strange couple. David smiled.

'We have an appointment with Diamond Jim Sullivan at 2.15,' said David in his polite voice.

'Ah, yes, Mr Sullivan has been expecting you,' the oriental girl replied. 'Please follow me.' They went through the door into a foyer with an elevator. The girl took them to the first floor and sat them down in a room full of black leather settees and chairs. The carpet was midnight blue and the walls were pink. A large desk was at the end of the room behind which was a swivel brown-hide chair in which sat a svelte business-suited middle-aged man. He was in his fifties. The suit was pin-striped, worn with a blue shirt and mauve tie. He stood up and motioned to them to sit down.

'You said you had a proposition for me. You mentioned that I had done business with a colleague of yours named Kara and I would be interested in what you had in mind.' He paused.

Kayley spoke as she took out the matching gems from a little silk bag and placed them before Diamond Jim on his desk.

'You may have these, which will be worth £1,000,000 on the open market, free of charge if you agree not to supply weapons and munitions to any of these three men.' David slid the three photos of Zak, Jay and Zadok over to Jim. He perused them thoughtfully for a few moments. Kayley spoke again, softly.

'They want twelve AK-47s, twenty-four Colt .45 pistols and fifty grenades – so our information tells us,' she continued.

'What makes you think I deal in munitions, young lady?' Jim asked tartly.

'Cut the crap, Sullivan, are you interested in £1,000,000 worth of jewellery or not?' David snarled at him. Jim said nothing. Then he took hold of the stones and examined them. He matched them together and saw the design of an island and a mainland on them as he held them together. He smiled. He gave a thin barracuda smile and looked up at them both.

'Excuse me a minute,' he said, then he pushed his telephone intercom and said into it.

'Send in Frankie Hayes, please, Miss Griffin.' Immediately an adjoining door opened and a thick-set black man came in, wearing a bright check suit with a black shirt and white tie.

'Come in, Francis,' said Diamond Jim. Then, he said to David and Kayley, 'Frankie is my munitions expert who deals exclusively with our sale of weapons and the like. Show the pictures to him, please. He will tell you if he has done business with any of the three gentlemen you seem concerned about.'

Frankie Hayes inspected the three photos for a short while himself. Then he said, 'Only this morning I sold them twelve AK-47s, twenty-four Colt .45's and fifty grenades. They went only two hours ago.'

'Damn them to hell,' David muttered. Kayley picked up the two gems and returned them to the silk bag quickly.

'However I heard them talking about sailing on a ship called *Ulysses* for the West Indies from 'D' wharf in New York harbour on Friday 19 August – sailing at 9 p.m.,' Frankie Hayes volunteered apologetically.

'If that is so,' David muttered to Kayley, 'then we have no time to lose. Thank you, gentlemen, for your co-operation. Goodbye.' They let themselves out quickly, leaving the puzzled gangsters looking bewildered.

Chapter Thirteen

A few days later Archimedes Ajax cut an imposing figure in his office at military headquarters in Kinshasa. He wore a khaki outfit consisting of a military jacket aflow with a general's epaulettes together with khaki slacks that were perfectly pressed. He wore a Sam Brown belt and he was smoking a large Havana cigar. The office was typically masculine. There was a mahogany six-drawer desk with green skiver top and a dark brown swivel chair behind it. There were pictures of Ajax in his Sandhurst days on the wall. He also had pictures of military uniforms and outfits adorning his four walls. Ajax was in a serious mood. He buzzed his intercom.

'Send in Lieutenant Colonel Sealey immediately,' he barked to his desk sergeant in the next room.

'Aye aye, sir!' came the reply from the frightened non-commissioned officer. Archimedes had this effect on people. He ruled by fear and no-one was immune.

About two minutes later Colonel Sealey knocked at the door.

'Enter,' shouted Ajax and Sealey walked in. He was shorter than his superior officer by a few inches but he was a fine figure of a man. He had the face of a bulldog, ruddy, with puckered veins in his cheeks. He walked with military precision, with a straight back and a sit-up-and-beg gait. His eyes were dark brown and he had eyebrows that met in the middle. His hair was brylcreemed straight back and he carried his cap in his hands. Archimedes changed his tack when his subordinate came in. They were old friends, used to each other's habits and mannerisms.

'Glad to see you, Stavros,' Ajax murmured.

'And you too, Archimedes,' Sealey addressed him informally and warmly.

'We must address the situation as it now stands,' Ajax went on. 'Sit down, Stavros, and we will discuss the situation.'

Sealey made himself comfortable on the seat facing Ajax's desk while Archimedes himself sat on his swivel chair. The two men looked at each other, both relaxed in each other's company. Then Ajax stood up; he seemed to fill the room with his height. He was a great bull of a man whose presence intimidated all but Lieutenant Colonel Stavros Sealey.

They had trained together at Sandhurst. Being black, they were subject to bullying and were called 'baboons' and 'coons' behind their backs. They forged a friendship even at that early stage and although Sealey was a Kenyan and Ajax from Zaire, when Ajax pushed through his FANC. Major Sealey was transferred to his unit, the Seventh Armoured Division in Kananga where Ajax promoted him to Lieutenant Colonel. Both men had masterminded the blitz on Africa for which Ajax was given all the glory. Sealey didn't mind being second-in-command; he had played second fiddle to a tough elder brother in his childhood and was better suited as a trusted lieutenant rather than rumbustious leader. It was a role that sat softly on his shoulders.

While Ajax blustered ahead it was Sealey who prodded and prompted his friend. The two men were good friends but Sealey was not as ruthless and bloodthirsty as his senior and he preferred it that way. Whilst Ajax secretly resented the whites (especially those in the RSA and Zimbabwe), Sealey saw that they were a necessary part of Africa's heritage; they were part and parcel of modern Africa. Sealey had appreciated the hard knocks the British army had given him whilst Ajax was full of bloodlust and hatred of the Europeans in Africa. Sealey did not share his misgivings, preferring to keep his own counsel over the issue in case he needed white allies in the future. Whatever else he was, Stavros Sealey was a realist and as such had more clarity of thought than Ajax.

Ajax pointed to a large map of Africa behind him and ushered Sealey to it. He gave him a hard ivory cane.

'Give me a briefing of the current position, Stavros. I have to go on SABCI television in an hour and I need to know the full picture.' Sealey moved like a panther to the giant map of Africa. He took overall control.

'President Zulelli has quashed all resistance in Namibia. However the Boers and rich whites in the RSA are up in arms about our coup. His tank divisions and infantry have declared a state of military law in Cape Town and Johannesburg. There is fighting between the poor blacks and the rich Europeans. Gangs of blacks from ghettos are ransacking and pillaging the more opulent areas in both cities. It seems to be a full-time job at present. Durban and Pretoria aren't far behind. There have been break-ins in factory complexes and a few fires have broken out there, too.'

'How large is Zulelli's complement in the RSA, Stavros?'

Sealey thought for a moment then he replied. 'He has enough troops and firepower to quell all unrest in Durban and Pretoria with full militia to assist other armies if he needs to, chief.'

Ajax acknowledged the use of his more accustomed title and beat his fingers on his table thoughtfully.

'Okay, we'll leave it for now. Tell me more, Stavros. I need the full picture.'

'Well, General Egberti in Zimbabwe is finding more unrest there between the moneyed white farmers and the poor blacks. It seems the revolution has affected the blacks as we thought it would. They are grasping their chance to rape, ransack and pillage. Bulewayo and Harare are hardest hit.' He paused for effect. Then he added. 'Shops, cinemas, hotels and schools have been particularly hard hit in the absence of Egberti's military presence. When the cat's away the mice will play.'

'Get him to send two of his crack units from Katanga to Bulewayo and Harare to discourage any more street violence. Tell him to capture the black ringleaders and make an example of them. It shouldn't take more than a few days at the most. If the natives are restless we'll just have to discourage them.' Ajax spoke curtly but succinctly to his aid. Sealey continued using the ivory cane as he pointed to the map of Africa.

'President Odinga of Kenya is encountering resistance in Somalia. Streetwise blacks are occupying mission halls and schools, that sort of thing. Nothing major but making Odinga deploy his armed forces at full strength. Nkomo of Nigeria is meeting with token resistance in Sierra Leone. Border skirmishes involving urban guerrillas are also occupying his troops.' He pointed to Sierra Leone and Somalia with his stick as he spoke.

Ajax was silent for a while. He moved to his chair, sitting

down as he spoke. 'Get on to both men and get them to use all possible firepower and military force to quell and destroy all resistance. And I mean destroy, Stavros. I want complete ruthlessness in both cases. We can't have unrest at all. Tell them to seize the ringleaders and make public examples of them. You know the drill, Stavros. Tell them I expect peace immediately.' Ajax referred to an infamous capture he had made some years before in Kisangani in Zaire. He had surrounded a school with black infants in it and totally destroyed it in a matter of a few hours. Ten teachers were murdered and three hundred children were annihilated in a bloody torturous battle. It had made headline news worldwide and Ajax had had to play down the incident to President Clinton and Tony Blair. Both men took out embargoes on arms and trade until Ajax rebuilt the school and redeployed new teachers and pupils in the new building.

'What else do I need to know about?' Ajax asked Sealey.

'Merely that RSA's Zulelli has deployed more of his troops to quell unrest in Senegal and Guinea in West Africa,' he said as he pointed to the two countries on his map.

Archimedes replied, 'What sort of unrest?'

'The usual, Archimedes. Poor black gangs devastating shops, hotels and civic centres. It is almost all over bar the shouting but I thought you ought to know.' Ajax nodded and smiled. When Archimedes smiled his charm was infectious. No one was immune. Not even Sealey. He smiled back. 'That is all,' he said and sat down.

'Good. I need to go on television in an hour or so. It is a TV film crew from South Africa and it is being shot in this office. It's going out all over Africa at 10 p.m. so I need to freshen up. Report to me at 0900 hours tomorrow and we will take it from there.' He saluted and the salute was returned.

Stavros Sealey knew when to speak and when to leave his master's presence. He walked to the door. Turning as he left, he said, 'Good luck for tonight, Archimedes.'

'Luck has nothing to do with it,' was the blunt reply. Sealey quit while he was ahead.

Three cameras were positioned around Ajax's huge desk. The map of Africa was nowhere to be seen. Spotlights warmed the whole scenario so that it was intensely hot and looked exactly what it was – a mobile television studio. The director barked orders to the cameramen and an assortment of make-up artists, production assistants, floor managers and hangers-on were fluttering around.

General Archimedes Ajax sat in his dark brown swivel chair. He looked the part.

Cool as a cucumber.

'Roll 'em!' The director yelled. The cameras started rolling.

'Good evening, fellow citizens of Africa,' Archimedes began. He paused for effect. 'We have seen fit to unify the whole of black Africa in the last few days. No longer do we have the Federation of National African Congress, which was effective in only parts of Africa, as you know. I am making this broadcast to tell you that we have a new conglomerate. A new state which we shall know as the United Black African Republic or UBAR.' The polished performance of Archimedes' statesmanship hid all presence of the megalomania that drove him. He was credible. Believable. Honest even. He smiled at the cameras as he spoke. Persuasively he purred through the television broadcast in such a way that no one doubted his integrity or authenticity. Yes, the Lion of Africa was seated on his throne.

Archimedes slept soundly that night.

But there were a lot of people all over Africa who didn't.

Chapter Fourteen

David used his contacts as a part-time policeman in London to get in touch with the appropriate organisation in New York. At first he met with scant success. Then a superintendent he had worked with told him that the Eighty-Ninth Precinct of the New York Police Department were hot on the heels of the mob themselves. David traced the Eighty-Ninth Precinct and met with little success when he spoke with the desk sergeant there.

'Superintendent Colson of Scotland Yard in London said that you were interested in nailing the Cosa Nostra,' he said. Suddenly the desk sergeant seemed attentive.

'Yeah... doesn't Jack know a superintendent in London by the name of Colson?' He called to a man serving on the desk with him.

'Sure does, Gus. He worked with him some years back in the UK. They ran a drugs bust together and became good pals,' came the reply.

'Wait a minute, sir,' the desk sergeant said while he phoned somebody. David didn't hear the conversation but he was asked to come inside and walk along the corridor inside the building. He and the New York Police Sergeant walked to an important door marked 'Captain J Markovich'. He knocked and they both went in. The sergeant introduced David to Captain Markovich who was on the phone but offered him a chair. David sat down.

The captain was engrossed in a long telephone conversation that seemed to David to last forever. Finally he put the phone down and said, 'Hi, I'm Jack Markovich. How can I help?'

David explained that he had worked with Superintendent Colson in London and that he had recommended the captain as someone hot on the heels of Diamond Jim Sullivan and the mob's activities. Markovich listened to him and said dryly, 'So what do you want me to do?'

David explained that the AK 47s, Colt .45s and grenades had

been sold to Zak, Jay and Zadok by Diamond Jim on the previous day, Thursday 18 August. Markovich seemed genuinely interested. He explained that the contraband was likely to be aboard the merchantman *Ulysses* docked at D Wharf in New York harbour. He stressed it was due to sail on Friday 19 August at 9 p.m. – today.

'What's in it for me and my people?' Markovich countered.

'If you catch these men with the munitions, you can make it stick by getting them to talk.'

'How?'

'You can grill them until they sing about getting the weapons from Frankie Hayes, Diamond Jim's right-hand man.' David let it sink in. 'If you play your cards right, you can make the bust stick. You can have Diamond Jim Sullivan in for possessing stolen weapons and drugs. Think what it'll do for your career. You're a captain now but it won't do your chances of promotion any harm. Especially if you bust his front, the Gold Arts jewellery store and find more contraband such as drugs. It'll be front page news in the *New York Times*. Think of the publicity – "New York captain breaks drug baron".' Captain Markovich played with a pen on his desk. He was pensive for thirty seconds, looking out of his office window. Then he became friendly towards David. He spoke in a conspiratorial tone.

'So this ship sails tomorrow at nine. And you believe the weapons are on it now. And you think Gold Arts jewellery is a front for drugs? We've been working a stake out on Gold Arts from the opposite side of the street and what you say holds water. The drugs come in from Colombia and if our officers are right the building is a place where Sullivan and his soldiers dispense the heroin to people in the employ of the mob. They circuit it in suitcases to pushers on the street. So far we've never caught them doing it. We have photographic evidence of comings and goings from our men. Getting in there would probably blow the case open for us. I head an operation called 'Operation Godfather' and this could be the lead we're looking for.' Markovich stopped for a minute to catch his breath. He looked out of the window again for some time then he said to David, 'Mr Marchbanks, I'll help you.'

'Call me David,' David replied. He relaxed and they both looked out of the window. Then the two men began to do some serious talking. Two hours and two hamburgers later, David Marchbanks walked out of the station with a confident gait to his step.

That afternoon Captain Markovich visited D Wharf with two black-and-white police cars containing three armed patrolmen. He walked up the gangplank of the *Ulysses*. She was a medium-sized freighter bound for the West Indies. Markovich asked for the captain.

Finally Captain Romero, a Greek Cypriot, invited him into his cabin. The sea captain was anxious to co-operate with the NYPD in any way he could.

'Markovich, NYPD, Captain. Did you undertake to take three men with you to the West Indies yesterday?'

'Yes I did,' Romero replied. 'Why the interest, sir?'

'Did they have any cargo with them, Captain?' Markovich asked.

'Why, yes. It's in No. 3 hold. In three wooden crates.'

'Can I see it?' Markovich continued, eyeing his patrolman meaningfully as he did. The patrolman smiled back at him knowingly.

'I'll take you to the cargo immediately, Lieutenant.'

'*Captain* Markovich of the Eighty-Ninth Precinct, *Captain*!' Markovich snapped.

'Of course, Captain Markovich. Follow me.' The ship's captain led them through passages to the inside door of a hold. He walked over to three crates and touched them with his feet.

'Those are they,' he nodded non-committally. Captain Markovich showed the sea captain his badge and then said to his patrolman.

'Open them up, Russ.'

The patrolman opened all three wooden cases. They found three AK-47s, twenty-four Colt .45s and fifty hand grenades.

'We'll take this, Captain Romero,' Markovich said. The sea captain shrugged.

'My pleasure. I don't ask questions. I always co-operate with the police, especially New York Police Department.'

'No sweat, Captain. We'll take this,' Markovich told Romero.

At five o'clock New York time, the two police cars were hidden in two adjoining warehouses. One before you got to the *Ulysses* on the right as you travelled along the quayside, and the second a hundred yards further along the quay. It was a light summer evening and sunlight covered the area. The shadow of the ship cut across the quayside. The warehouse filled the wharf fifty yards inland.

Captain Markovich and one patrolman lay in wait behind a door of the *Ulysses* next to her gangplank on A Deck. Both the captain and his colleague were armed: the former with a pistol and the latter with a rifle. The rifle peeked out of the doorway on the deck of the ship.

About a hundred yards further along the wharf the two other armed patrolmen sat, waiting for any sign of life just inside the warehouse door. They were not alone. Next to them were David Marchbanks and Kayley in her wheelchair.

David was armed with a pistol but Kayley had no weapon even though she was a crack shot. She had shot Dik Dik and Thompson's Gazelle in Kenya whilst on holiday and she was every bit as good as Markovich's riflemen. But Markovich was calling the shots so she was unarmed. She sat next to David, about ten feet from the two cops. The atmosphere was tense. The two men smoked Lucky Strikes. David did not. They waited patiently as the sun began to fall in the sky. The New York skyline became a silhouette.

Six o'clock came and went. With the exception of two seamen kissing goodbye to their girlfriends, there was no activity on the quayside. Seamen walked about all over the ship, tightening ropes and going about their business oblivious to the ambush about to take place.

Then, at five minutes past seven, a taxi arrived at the quayside about fifty yards from the gangplank. Three men got out of it and one paid the driver. They seemed apprehensive and looked around them. The tallest man looked at the *Ulysses* from the wharf. It was a sun-drenched evening and the light bound off of a rifle barrel. The man's eyes narrowed. He peered up at the ship. Suddenly the glint of the rifle flashed into his eyes. He turned fifty yards from the gangplank to his two friends. They got into deep conversation. David strained as he watched Zak, Jay and Zadok huddled together deep in conversation. He wondered what they'd do next.

Then they walked along the quay towards the gangplank. It took them thirty seconds. Both marksmen viewed the three men. They were briefed by Captain Markovich to capture, not to kill.

Suddenly the three men broke into a run along the quayside past the front of the ship. Both sets of riflemen fired warning shots over their heads.

'Stop or we'll shoot!' Markovich bellowed. The three men ignored him, running towards the end of the quay. Shots rang out again, aimed closer now but not close enough to wound or kill the three men. Suddenly Zak, Jay and Zadok began bobbing and weaving as they ran, making themselves a difficult target for the riflemen on the ship and in the warehouse. They aimed high and the shots rang out in the vicinity, ricocheting as they did so. By now the three men were running at full tilt. They were well past the warehouse where the policemen stood about fifty yards down the quayside. Both sets of riflemen were awaiting further instructions, which never came.

'Damn! Damn! Damn!' shouted Captain Markovich as the three men reached the end of the quay. They dived right into the Hudson, fifty feet beneath the wharf. David and the two officers chased after them as fast as they could.

David reached the edge first. He was fitter than the older, fatter men. They followed him and together they stood looking into the sea.

There was no sign of the three men in the water. No heads to view. Absolutely nothing.

Thirty seconds later Captain Markovich ran to the quay's edge to join his men. 'Bang goes our chance to bust Diamond Jim Sullivan, fellows,' he muttered more to himself than anyone.

'Well, you've got the weapons. On the strength of those you can enter Diamond Jim's Gold Arts jewellery store, and see if you can find some heroin, Captain.' David commiserated.

The other man shrugged dismissively in reply.

'But think of what I could have done had we caught these

punks,' he said looking into the sunset. The sun was fast disappearing. They all walked forlornly back to the hidden vehicles.

'I guess *something* is better than nothing,' Captain Markovich philosophised. At least he could enter Diamond Jim Sullivan's front now. The hooter on the *Ulysses* sounded deeply into the evening air. The night seemed cold to all of them now.

Chapter Fifteen

Zak, Jay and Zadok were sitting in the yellow taxi cab as it made its way through the busy city streets. It was a case of stop-start, stop-start. The three men said little. They were preoccupied with the thought of travelling on the *Ulysses* to the West Indies. The streets were still busy. People who had been working late hurried along the pavement. A hot dog stand did steady business on one street corner. New York was always busy. A tramp with his trusty dog looked in at the taxi as it stopped at some traffic lights. The taxi's back window was open; it was quite hot. An August night in New York.

'Buddy, can you spare a dollar?' The street tramp asked. The three men ignored him as the taxi moved on. Left behind, he waved a theatrical fist at the disappearing cab. They sped through the streets. It was close to seven o'clock. The sun was still setting and Zak had to shield his eyes from the glare.

'I suspect a trap. I feel there could be a police ambush,' he said to the other two men. Zak, although he was more evil than good in his lifestyle, still possessed second sight. He still had premonitions as most Atlanteans did.

'What do you mean?' Zadok queried.

'Don't know. Just feel we could be set up,' he replied. The taxi turned into the harbour complex. They travelled along past myriad quays and warehouses. Zak felt very uneasy. But he tried to hide his suspicions from his two cronies for fear of startling them. They were followers not leaders. He was the natural leader and always had been.

The taxi finally turned into D Wharf. It was two hundred yards long. The driver drove at a walking pace. Finally the cab came to a halt about twenty feet from the gangplank of the *Ulysses*. The three men slowly got out. Jay and Zadok had let off steam by having a few pints of Budweiser. Zak had not. He had to keep a clear mind. As he got out he took a long leisurely look around him. He saw two warehouses to the right. The corrugated door of one was open. Zak scrutinised the opening. He thought he saw a shadow. Was it a man? Could he be imagining it? No, he needed to keep his nerve. His intuition never failed him and now he was very suspicious. *It could be a man*, he thought to himself. There was a hint of movement just behind the door. Zak was alert to it. He didn't let on to the others as they sloppily alighted from the yellow taxi cab. They were conversing happily but Zak was wide awake. Then he fixed his eyes on the ship itself. He surveyed the gangplank at a forty degree angle running up to the ship's deck. About ten feet to its left was an open door which looked highly suspicious to Zak. Why was it open? Ship's doors on deck were always closed. Yet this one was open. It seemed fishy. Zak fixed his eyes on the door suspiciously. All his senses told him something was up. He couldn't put his finger on it but something was definitely amiss. Zak felt it deep inside – he felt danger. Why was he so suspicious? He didn't know exactly, but his intuition rarely failed him.

As Zak was viewing the door something glinted in the sunlight. It caught his eye. He blinked, adjusting his eyesight as he did. He narrowed his eyes to take in the range of place where the flash of light had come from. Was he imagining it? No, it definitely was there.

As he narrowed his eyes he saw it. A gun barrel. Sticking out of the doorway. Zak peered at the doorway. Was he mistaken? He thought for a moment. No, he wasn't mistaken! The gun barrel moved about two inches in the evening sunlight.

Zak turned casually around the face the quayside. It was about fifty yards to the end of the wharf. To the water. To safety. He turned back to the gangplank to confirm his suspicions. Jay and Zadok were talking happily to one another on the quay, oblivious to the danger.

Zak looked again. Seriously this time. A long lingering look at the open doorway. No, it wasn't his eyes playing tricks on him. It definitely was a gun barrel. The sunlight shone on it again and Zak was certain.

So it was an ambush. Somehow the police were on to them. Zak didn't start to wonder how.

He thought fast.

Keep a cool head. Find a way out of this. Steady, boy, steady.

Zak motioned to the other two as the yellow cab drove quickly away. He tried to be as casual as possible. Keep your nerve. Keep calm. Lowering his voice as if to tell a dirty joke, Zak spoke to the other two.

'There is a gun pointed at us, guys. We are being ambushed. Keep calm and do what I tell you, right?'

Jay and Zadok immediately came to their senses. They, too, knew what it was like to run from the law.

'When I give the signal I want you to run as fast as you can to the end of the quay. Don't run straight; weave as you run so as to be a difficult target to hit. Is that clear?' Both men nodded, alive in their mutual fear. Zak waited a few seconds, then he hissed silently.

'Go!'

All three men began to bob and weave at a pace along the quayside. It took them ten yards to reach full speed. Gun shots rang out. It was over their heads. The crack of rifle bullets whipped at their senses. They carried on running.

They were zigzagging along the cold hard stone. The noise of the gunfire reached them but they took no notice. Then when they were about fifteen yards from the edge they heard a man's high pitched voice scream at them.

'Stop or we'll shoot!' the voice yelled but Zak, Jay and Zadok couldn't hear it properly. They were running for all they were worth. Fifteen yards to go. They still moved around as they ran.

Ten yards...

It seemed like ten minutes. Time stood still.

Five yards to go.

All three men were running at full tilt. Oblivious to all around them. Gunfire cracked over their heads. It didn't seem to be near them.

Then they reached the edge.

All three jumped into the lukewarm harbour. They felt a sense of weightlessness as they were in mid air. Then they crashed into the water and disappeared from sight. All three men were, of course, expert swimmers having once been ambitious. They still possessed the ability to swim underwater for long periods of time. They swam expertly down about thirty feet. The bubbles of air rose to the surface. Other than that there was no trace of them. They swam powerfully underwater motivated by fear. Zak was the most powerful swimmer but the other two weren't far behind. When Zak had been swimming for approximately two minutes he motioned to the others to swim to the surface. Jay and Zadok obeyed their leader. When they reached the surface they were two hundred yards from the wharf's edge. In the evening light they could just make out the silhouettes of people standing, rifles in hand, peering out to the open sea.

They were too far out to be seen. Zak shouted to the other two. 'We'll swim to the shore, lads.'

Jay and Zadok nodded back to him. So they swam on the surface through the half mile of water.

It took them fifty minutes. It would have taken a human being twice the time at least. It was about five minutes to eight when Zak and the other two crawled onto the beach of Staten Island.

Zak threw himself onto the surface. All three took time to get their breath back. Then at last Zak spoke for all of them.

'We got away. But we've lost our weapons. We've missed the *Ulysses* for sure. Jewel will be furious with us for failing him a second time.' He shuddered at the thought. The two other men nodded in agreement.

'At least we've escaped with our lives,' Zak said as the sun disappeared over the horizon.

Markovich and his men drove back in silence to their police headquarters. A cab took David and Kayley to Trump Tower Hotel for the night.

Markovich said little during the journey. He was preoccupied with the fact that the three men had escaped. Still, he had the weapons which would give him a warrant to search Diamond Jim's residence. Perhaps he'd be lucky. There had been very little he could have done to change the circumstances. Had he ordered his men to shoot to kill he would have had three dead men and worse than that, he'd be guilty of homicide. No, he'd done all he could in the circumstances.

'You couldn't have got them, Captain,' said his driver, reading his thoughts. 'They must have seen us. They ran so quickly and we weren't quick enough. Some you win, some you lose, I guess.' Captain Markovich silently agreed with his patrolman.

'Take the weapons in and book them in to the holding bay. Then you can go home, Kopanski.'

Kopanski said nothing and they drove back in silence to the police station. The evening air was humid. It got very muggy in New York at this time of year. Markovich went home to his wife and to a nice evening meal and bed. He'd had enough for one day.

He slept like a log.

The next day, Saturday, Captain Markovich took two black-and-whites to Gold Arts Jewellers. It was ten in the morning. The day was very hot. Humid, not dry. Markovich was sweating with excitement. This was the break he'd been looking for. He was glad he'd listened to the limey cop. He liked the kid. They did things differently in England but basically it was the same thing: a constant struggle against crime. 'Operation Godfather' had been in action for over a year now and with any luck he'd be able to pin something on Diamond Jim Sullivan. He'd been waiting a long time for that. These thoughts were going through his mind as the police car sped through the crowded New York streets. They arrived at Gold Arts. Markovich and his men got out, and entered the shop. Markovich showed the oriental girl his badge.

'I've come to see Mr Sullivan,' he explained. She motioned to the door behind her. The four men went through to Diamond Jim's office. Jim wasn't expecting them. Markovich changed his tune for Diamond Jim who was seated at his office desk.

'Morning, Sullivan, I've got a warrant to search your premises,' he barked to the other man. He tossed the warrant onto Jim's desk. Jim didn't look at it. He stared at the four policemen.

'Johnson, Patricks, go and search upstairs. David, start searching here.' Markovich was dressed in civilian clothes. His officers wore NYPD uniform. He sat down in a guest chair directly opposite Diamond Jim. The two men glared at one another.

'We have taken possession of stolen weapons which were sold

to three men by you, Sullivan. Twelve Russian AK-47s, twenty-four Colt .45 pistols and fifty grenades. We have photos of it.' The smug smile on Diamond Jim's face disappeared. He wasn't quite as sure of himself as he had been when they had entered.

'What do you want, Markovich? I'm clean. I run a respectable jewellery shop her and you know it,' he blustered. Markovich said nothing. He was looking at Davis who was opening cupboards and drawers inside the office as they spoke. There was a grey aluminium case beside Jim's desk. Davis was working his way around the room. He came to the case. He put it on Jim's desk and tried to open it. It was locked.

'Open it, Sullivan!' Markovich ordered. Diamond Jim self-consciously put a key into the lock. He, too, was sweating now. The cat was out of the bag. The lock clicked. Davis opened it. It was full of polythene bags of white powder. Davis and Captain Markovich looked knowingly at one another. They had struck gold!

Markovich reached for the penknife in his pocket. Slowly but meticulously he cut a hole in one bag. Then with his forefinger he put some of the white powdery substance to his lips and tasted it. It tasted sour. Bingo.

'Heroin,' he said. 'Sullivan, I'm arresting you for possession of heroin. You are coming down with me to the station.' Then for the first time that morning Captain Jack Markovich allowed himself a smile.

'Operation Godfather' had had a big break. He'd see if he could break Diamond Jim Sullivan down at the station during interrogation. He'd have to be quick, mind you, because it wouldn't be long before Sullivan had his attorney bail him out.

Still, it was a good day and tomorrow was his day off!

Chapter Sixteen

'Doctor Shasa to Omar Ward. Doctor Shasa, please,' the receptionist's voice sounded crisply over the loudspeaker in the heat of the African afternoon.

Victor Shasa was walking along the corridor in Leopoldville Hospital in Kinshasa when he heard the announcement. It was five o'clock and it had been a long day for Victor. He had come in as normal at eight o'clock. With the exception of a light curry at lunchtime in the hospital canteen, Victor had been on the go all day. *I'll see what she wants*, Victor thought to himself as he moved faster between the wards. He was tired and he knew it. These damned hospital administrators didn't know the pressure consultants were put under these days, reasoned Victor irritably. Slowly, he made his way through the maze of corridors.

Victor reached Omar Ward and he walked into the Sister's office. Sister Cicero was a broad, well-built woman who was used to taking responsibility for people's lives. She had been at Leopoldville for seven years, and there was little that got past her in the hospital.

'I want you to look at a patient, Victor,' she said to Doctor Shasa abruptly.

'What's the problem?' Victor enquired politely. She sat down and breathed a sigh of mock-relief. Emily Cicero was a nice woman. Fat and fifty, but nevertheless an attractive woman for all that.

'We've had a young soldier admitted from Kinshasa Barracks this afternoon, Victor. And I'm worried, I don't mind admitting it. He has diarrhoea and vomiting and a temperature of 104 degrees. He keeps slipping in and out of consciousness. I'm afraid we're going to lose him.'

'When did it start?' Victor asked her.

'Today. The MO at Kinshasa Barracks has five soldiers in his sick bay already with similar symptoms. This boy has been ill for five days, so he says, but it was only today that his temperature went up and he became delirious.'

Victor assessed the situation. He was the senior consultant at the hospital and he was used to problems being thrown at him willy-nilly. He thought for a few moments. Sister Cicero told him of the medication the MO had prescribed. He frowned.

'Take him off that,' he snapped angrily. Young doctors always used the medicine most in vogue. Not Victor. He relied on his tried and trusted methods, which had proved to be useful time and time again. Many a time Victor had shown up young housemen for what they really were. Just puppies playing with medicine. Victor knew better.

'Where is he?'

'I've put him in a private room,' Sister replied.

'I'll take a look at him,' Victor said.

Victor walked into the young soldier's room. He was moaning unconsciously. Sweat covered his face. The bedclothes were all over the place. Victor appraised the situation. A nurse was sitting next to the bed, keeping a responsible vigil.

'What's his blood pressure?'

'One twenty over eighty, Doctor Shasa.'

Victor nodded. He looked at the boy's eyes, then prodded his stomach, concentrating as he did so. He took the medical report at the bottom of the bed and read it slowly. He was nothing if not methodical. He put it back, thanked the nurse then walked out of the room back to Sister Cicero.

'What do you think it is, Sister?'

'It could be Crohn's Disease, irritable bowel syndrome or colitis,' she offered.

'That doesn't explain the high temperature and the loss of consciousness though.'

'True.'

'May I use your phone?'

'Certainly.' Sister Cicero excused herself and left the little office, leaving Victor all to himself. He picked up the phone.

'Give me Kinshasa Barracks. Doctor Kamila please.' Victor waited while the receptionist connected him.

'Shasa here, Consultant at Leopoldville. What do you think is the matter with your patients, Doctor?'

Kamila welcomed the straight talk and returned the compliment in kind.

'I haven't met anything like it, Doctor. I've worked in the tropics for thirteen years and before that in Britain. It seems like some kind of 'flu virus that affects the stomach and makes the patient delirious. How's our boy?'

'Comfortable. How many others have you got in that apology of yours you call a sick bay?'

'We had five this morning. But I've had three more with high temperatures this afternoon. That makes eight in all. Then there's yours...' He hesitated. 'I'll let you know if we need to transfer them to you, Doctor.'

'Thank you, Sam. Keep me posted. Ciao,' he said. The phone clicked and Victor looked absent-mindedly out of the window. Then he reached for Sister Cicero's medical almanac and consulted it over killer viruses. He sat in her office for ten minutes, boning up on the symptoms of the new patient. Then he looked at his watch. It was six o'clock. He had a dinner date at eight. He waved to the sister in the ward. She came back to her office.

'I'm going home now, Sister. I'll leave my pager on in case you need me or the situation gets worse. Put him on Dioralyte. I hope the virus breaks and his temperature falls. Goodnight.' Victor walked to his office, took off his white overall, locked his office door and headed for the car park. Yes, it had been a hell of a day. He needed sleep, not dinner.

At Port Elizabeth Hospital in Pretoria, Jake Francis was encountering a similar dilemma. This time a woman corporal of the Kimberley Lancers, one of the RSA's finest regiments, had been brought in by ambulance.

She had been vomiting and she had diarrhoea. She had a temperature of 101 degrees and she drifted in and out of consciousness from minute to minute. He had her on a drip.

Jake was worried.

He'd seen the flu epidemic in Hong Kong in the fifties when

he was a young intern. In forty years as a doctor this was the first thing he'd seen that came as near to it in its worse state. The girl couldn't have been more than twenty-four. Yet she seemed to be hanging on to life by a thread. Jake's expression was grim. He'd talked to the medical officer at Krugersdorp Barracks, Pretoria. The story was typical. The MO had fourteen other people in his military hospital who weren't quite so serious. But the matter was beginning to appear severe.

Fifteen people with a dangerous virus, Jake thought to himself. He rang a colleague in Durban who was fighting the same condition there. This time there were six delirious patients with exactly the same symptoms: diarrhoea, vomiting and a high temperature. What could it be? Jake frowned. It wasn't like him to be puzzled.

In Machako, just outside Nairobi, was the military headquarters of the Seventh Kenya Rifles. There was confusion and panic. One soldier who, had diarrhoea and vomiting and a temperature of 103, had died. He had become delirious just before he died. It had been a quick death. The Medical Officer, Colonel Nyashi, had not been prepared for it. He had been in the Kenyan army for five years. Before that he had trained and practised in the Royal Free Hospital in London, England. As soon as he had further cases he transferred his patients to Hope Hospital in Kenyatta Drive in Nairobi. He had three more.

In Hope Hospital Doctor Tutu kept all three patients in quarantine. They were kept under surveillance by his nursing staff. One solider spoke incoherently. He was particularly bad. Tutu did his best. He felt the outbreak was some sort of fatal influenza bug. But he was unsure. It was outside his experience in all his years of medical practice. Doctor Tutu didn't know what to do for the three men who seemed to be teetering on the brink of death. In desperation he picked up the telephone. It was very hot that day and Tutu himself was sweating with nervousness.

'Get me Leopoldville Hospital in Kinshasa, Zaire, please,' he told the receptionist curtly.

'Putting you through,' she purred.

When he got through, he asked for Victor Shasa, an old friend whom he'd met at a medical conference in Frankfurt, Germany, some years before. They had become firm friends. Their friendship was based on a mutual respect for the knowledge each had of medicine.

'Victor? Jonas Tutu here.'

'Hello, Jonas. How can I help you?'

'We've had a strange influenza bug here at Hope Hospital,' he started. 'It's all diarrhoea and vomiting with high temperatures. The patient becomes delirious and slips in and out of consciousness.' Victor listened to his friend as he described the exact symptoms he was seeing at Kinshasa. They talked for some time. Neither were conversant with the virus and both were alarmed by its power.

'It's killed one person already,' Jonas Tutu told his friend. 'It seems to be devastating once it takes hold.'

'I know, Jonas, I know,' Victor replied. Of the two men Victor Shasa was the senior in medical experience but both were used to the diseases in Africa. This was different.

Both men were dismayed – what was this killer virus?

Zak, Jay and Zadok slept on the beach at Staten Island. It was night. The sun had set. The swim had sapped their strength. Even though they were fit, they needed to recharge their batteries. At about midnight they decided to go. So they clambered up from the beach and into the city. It was fairly dark and none of the men knew the way. As they walked slowly along the streets their clothes dried in the night air.

They heard a noise.

It was the sound of raised voices and quite a clatter. There seemed to be quite a few people. Perhaps it was some drunks going home from a bar. The noise got louder. The three men felt slightly threatened by the shouting and laughter. They were tired and the last thing they wanted was trouble.

'What is it?' Jay asked.

'Don't know,' Zak replied.

They continued to walk carefully along the lit street. As they walked along the pavement, they saw a procession of youths in the distance, coming their way. All three men were tired and weak.

The procession was about twenty in strength. It was a meeting of the Brownsville Buffaloes, a New York teenage gang. The boys had flick-knives, clubs, chains and hammers. One carried a mallet. The boys were about fifty yards away. They were looking for trouble. A fight gave them all street cred and increased the profile of the gang.

In the dark they saw three men silhouetted. They were ready to rumble. Ricardo was the leader of the gang. Tony was right-hand man. Both boys narrowed their eyes as they saw their quarry.

'We'll take these dudes,' Ricardo snarled.

'Right, boss, we're ready for a rumble. We've got our battle dress on and all our weapons. We shouldn't have much trouble with these punks. Are you all ready?' Tony asked. A chorus of agreement hit the New York air and the gang began to approach the three tired men. They were twenty yards away. Zak, Jay and Zadok were bigger than the teenage hoodlums but they were tired from the energy they had exerted in their getaway from the police five hours previously.

The gang tentatively surrounded the three men. There was an awkward silence.

'Come on, lads, we don't want any trouble,' Zak pleaded with them, anxious to avoid a confrontation.

'You've come across a ceremonial meeting of the Brownsville Buffaloes, man, and we own this turf. Understand?' Ricardo spat out the words aggressively. Tony swung a bicycle chain around ominously. *They mean business*, thought Zak.

'Separate,' he told the other two. And Jay and Zadok did exactly that.

There were twenty of the street kids. They were mean and fit. Some were high on smack. That made them more dangerous. About ten or so kids surrounded each man. This could get nasty. The sheer weight of numbers made the odds impossible for Zak, Jay and Zadok. They began reluctantly to fight.

It got grisly. Ricardo launched into Zak with frenzy. The flick-knife blade swished through the air. It caught Zak on his arm and drew blood. Zak aimed a punch at Ricardo. He missed and lost his footing. Quick as lightning, Ricardo put his right arm around Zak's shoulders and stabbed him in the back. Zak slid to the ground, gurgling with pain.

Jay and Zadok fared no better. A bicycle chain knocked Jay unconscious. A gang member drew a pistol and shot him through the head. Zadok was clubbed over the head with a baseball bat. He fell to the ground, face down. Fast Eddy shot him in the back of the head.

They had killed all three.

Honour had been done that night. Carefully, all twenty members carried the dead bodies into the night. When they got to the beach they tossed them into the sea from a nearby pier. The three bodies floated on the surface of the midnight water. The moon shone on the solid shapes as they floated in the bay.

Chapter Seventeen

The virus grew monstrously. It hit the shanty towns in South Africa particularly hard. Cape Town, Port Elizabeth, Johannesburg and East London as well as Pretoria and Durban were particularly bad. It seemed to hit the blacks like flies. They all had the similar symptoms: diarrhoea and vomiting together with a high temperature. The doctors requisitioned civil buildings and schools to cope with the intake. There were ten deaths in Johannesburg. Durban lost fifteen people. Pretoria's death count was seventeen. Cape Town had twenty deaths. Zaire fared no better. Kinshasa suffered twenty deaths; Kananga, fourteen; Mbuji-Mayi, twelve and Kisangani, nine.

In Kenya, Nairobi sustained fourteen deaths and Mombasa, eleven. The virus respected no one. All were susceptible to it. The doctors were baffled by it. No one could contain it. It took no prisoners.

Kinshasa was the headquarters of the United Black African Republic, or UBAR as it was known colloquially. As head of UBAR, Archimedes Ajax was notified of proceedings. Victor Shasa phoned him personally.

'We are sitting on a possible epidemic,' he told Ajax.

'I know, Victor,' Ajax said. Archimedes knew Victor Shasa well. He had treated Ajax personally for the past fifteen years. The men were firm friends. Victor respected Archimedes for his drive and ambition whereas Ajax secretly respected Victor for his total understanding of humanity and the disease that was hitting Africa so badly. Victor Shasa was a champion of the poor and oppressed. The pair had met many years ago at a London party when both were students. They'd hit it off immediately. Although Victor privately disapproved of Ajax's ruthlessness when he was in power, he never dared voice it publicly. Ajax cut down anything and anyone in his way. Victor knew his type only too well.

'What do you want me to do?' Ajax continued.

'Can you get the best medical brains from Europe to help, Archimedes?'

'My subordinates can get American, British and German specialists involved if that is what you want, Victor.'

'I think we need to keep it under wraps at the moment. Don't you?'

'I have a television interview this week. I'll put people's minds at rest. For the moment anyway.' Ajax rung off. He turned to Stavros Sealey.

'We'll swear our respective Heads of State to secrecy for the moment,' he reflected. 'Get on to it, Stavros.' Stavros nodded. There was no sense in letting everyone in Africa get into a panic. Still, Archimedes was worried.

He picked up his private phone and instructed his secretary to get the Health Minister to contact Washington, London and Bonn to send their respective specialists in the virus. They conversed for a while as Ajax explained the nature of the virus to her.

'How many deaths have we?' he asked Sealey. Sealey referred to his clipboard.

'There are a hundred and eight at the moment, chief. If I were you, I'd think seriously about addressing the continent about it. You have a press bulletin tomorrow in Cape Town. Don't you remember? It's a United Black African Republic press conference aimed at the unification of black Africa. Now that fighting has stopped everywhere you need to put everything on a firmer footing. This would put you across as a humane leader concerned for the welfare of his people. I can see the paper headlines now – Archimedes: "Lion of Africa cares for his people". It would be a good political move, especially after all the bloodshed and fighting.' Stavros stopped speaking, sensing that he had Ajax's attention. Of the two he was always the most level-headed. He was the power behind the throne. In reality that was the way Stavros Sealey liked it. The bloodshed and fighting had stopped two days ago and Ajax was booked to make a publicity statement declaring that Africa was now at peace and ready to move forward under his benevolent rule and oversight. Deep down those who knew him feared Ajax rather than loved him. This was a ploy to put him over as a father figure who was concerned for his people.

Saddam Hussein had done it in Iraq. Chancellor Kohl was considered the protector of unified Germany. Mitterand had come across as a humane leader in France. Clinton, of course, held sway in the US. He'd done so well he had run into his second term. This was Stavros' and Archimedes' plan for the trans-African television broadcast. To show a different side to the President of the United Black African Republic. It had been a smart move.

Until the virus had struck. The damned virus. Unless...

'Yes, Stavros, we could turn it to our advantage. I could come across to the continent as a benevolent servant of black and European Africa. People would see me in a new light.'

'It could work,' Stavros prompted, sensing he had Ajax in his clutches. He always teed Ajax up, letting him believe it had all been his idea. Stavros, like Christ, Mohammed and Ghandi before him, was a great teacher: one who sowed the seed of what was needed to be done and made the person who listened think it was his or her own idea. Ajax was putty in his hands.

'I think it would be an excellent move. Get my spin doctors to work on a new speech. Something rousing like Churchill might have said during the war. Let's turn this into our advantage, Stavros!'

'OK, chief.' There was a smile on Stavros's face.

June Champion was forty-five. She was going for her daily jog along the coast. It was six in the morning. June liked to jog before the rest of Staten Island woke up. At six the world was hers. She loved the quietness of the day. She ran three miles from her apartment and back. It didn't take her long and there was very little traffic on the roads. The streets were deserted. This was the time she was happiest. She could think of all the problems of the day as she ran. She wore a white sweatshirt with navy blue velvet running bottoms and sunglasses to hide the glare of the sun. Today was Monday. She was having a luncheon engagement with a girlfriend. She'd wear her pin-striped power suit and perhaps be lavish with her cosmetics. Anthea would be impressed with that. They'd have a good gossip. Anthea, her friend, was going through a rough time with her partner.

June had a new boyfriend. They'd have lots to talk about. These thoughts were going through June's mind as she ran at a canter.

Running along the coast she neared her turning point – a seventy-foot pier. June ran up to the end of the pier as part of her run. It was here that she turned to run back to her apartment. As she ran in the morning air her attention was caught by three logs floating on the water.

Or were they logs?

She ran closer to the water's edge. She noticed that they appeared to be human bodies. June froze. They appeared to be floating beneath the end of the pier. June stopped. She was shocked. She pulled herself together and came to her senses. She leaned over the pier itself to get a better view. There were definitely three bodies floating facedown in the sea. June became alarmed. She reached for her mobile phone and dialled 911.

'Which service do you require, ma'am?' came the polite operator's voice.

'Police. I've seen three dead bodies floating in the harbour.' June gave them the location details and ran back to her apartment. It spoiled her day.

'Are these the men?' Captain Jack Markovich asked David and Kayley. He passed three identikit pictures of the men to them. New York Harbour Police had collected the bodies, which were taken to the morgue. Identikit photos were passed round each police station. As soon as Markovich saw the three photos, he called David and Kayley.

They sat in his office drinking coffee from paper cups. Markovich's eyes did not leave his guests' faces. Kayley and David viewed the pictures silently. Then David said slowly, 'Yes. It's them alright. What happened to them? Where were they found?'

'One was knifed in the back. The other two were shot through the head at close range,' Markovich announced. His voice, though outwardly caustic, was full of regret. However long Captain Jack Markovich worked for the New York Police Department it would never be long enough for him to get used to the senseless loss of life he was so often forced to witness.

'My guess is that they swam from the quay to land at Staten Island. It probably took a lot out of them. It looks as if they ran into one of the teenage gangs that frequent the city. They were probably outnumbered and killed. Could have been a ritual gang murder, we'll never know.'

'You are the professional,' Kayley said gently to Markovich. 'We do know that it is Zak, Jay and Zadok definitely.'

'We'll put officers on the case but my suspicion is that we'll never find the perpetrators. Whatever the outcome we can't pin it on Diamond Jim Sullivan and his boys. No proof. No evidence to link him to the deaths,' observed Markovich tartly.

David and Kayley excused themselves and returned to their hotel. Both were sad. Any death is a shame; let alone gruesome killings. Kayley shuddered. David put a hand round her shoulder as they reached their suite at Trump Tower. It took the wind out of their sails.

They took lunch in their suite and discussed their next move now that Zak, Jay and Zadok were dead. Their mission had been accomplished – albeit by someone else.

More weapons would be taken for Jewel and his crew to use upon the city of Atlantis.

'How many dead?' Dr Heinrich Brandt, a German physician, asked.

'Over a thousand. Over the whole continent anyway,' replied Victor Shasa.

'And how many are hospitalised?' Dr Pat Kopanski enquired. He was a Washington medical advisor just arrived from the US.

'At the last count we had approximately three and a half thousand,' Victor answered.

'How quick is the virus to claim mortalities?' Dr Benjamin McTaggart, one of Britain's best medical brains, queried.

'Anything from five hours to three days,' Victor said. They were sitting in Victor Shasa's home in Kinshasa. They formed a medical committee aimed at foiling the virus. All three men had just arrived from their respective countries. They had been sent by Britain, Germany and the US as representatives chosen at cabinet level in reply to Ajax's cry for assistance. Each man had a fine reputation for medical science in his respective country.

With the exception of Brandt, who had worked in South Africa, neither of the men knew Africa very well. They'd holidayed there but they were unaware of the squalid conditions that led to the spreading of a virus. Kopanski had got his reputation working with AIDS victims in San Francisco. McTaggart had battled with HIV Positive patients in central London in his own clinic. Everyone seemed baffled at the way the virus had taken off in the three days since Ajax and Sealey had tabulated the death toll at 108.

Ajax had deferred his broadcast on the basis that the bug was spreading widely in all directions. The poverty in the RSA, Kenya and Zaire could not be helping whatever was causing the virus to spread. Nobody knew where it came from. It had just snowballed. It was no respecter of persons. There had been some European deaths. Even in the opulent homes of South Africa people had contracted the disease.

It was fast becoming an epidemic.

Ajax and Colonel Sealey had flown down to Cape Town to give his 'Lion of Africa' broadcast, casting him in a good and humane light.

Archimedes sat being made up by a make-up artist just before it was time to go on air. He felt relaxed and ebullient as he sat in the small make-up room. The girl cooed over him as she accentuated his bulbous features. Archimedes was impatient for it to start. Patience had never been his strong suit. He was a man of action. He was not good at playing diplomatic waiting games. Statesmanship did not sit lightly on his shoulders. He was a military man, not a natural politician. He envied those who were cordial and diplomatic but he secretly despised them. He was having a crash-course in diplomacy now!

He entered the studio and sat facing the cameras. Stavros Sealey entered. He called Ajax.

'Yes?' said Ajax curtly.

'There are a thousand dead, chief. I thought you ought to know. You need to be calm and persuasive. Let everybody know how much you care about the welfare and state of the continent of Africa.'

'The Lion of Africa must purr to his lion cubs,' Ajax shot at his assistant.

'Exactly, Archimedes, just right. Show the benevolent side of yourself. Thousands of people must see your compassion. Keep it simple and keep it sentimental. OK?' Ajax nodded. The director shouted 'Action!' and they were on air.

Archimedes Ajax became a different animal the moment the cameras were on him. He was suave, persuasive and gentle at the same time. He seemed entirely plausible. Like all dictators he believed completely that what he was saying was true and accurate. He came over well on camera.

The broadcast lasted ten minutes and was seen by millions all over Africa, and to the rest of the world on satellite.

'As you may know, we have in Africa a virus which is striking our people, especially in the poorer areas. We have a medical task force from the West which is fighting the bug. Its symptoms include vomiting, diarrhoea and high temperatures. This causes delirium and unconsciousness, and in some cases, death. Needless to say, we are combating this dreadful disease with every weapon in our medical armoury. Be reassured we will nip it in the bud. We shall not sleep until we have beaten it, people of the United Black African Republic. Rest assured that your future is safe in our hands.'

He finished speaking, and they came off air. The credits rolled and Archimedes walked out of the studio.

As he sat in the back of his black limousine taking him to his protected hotel, he muttered to Stavros Sealey, 'Christ, Stavros, I hope our medical brains can lick this thing.'

'They will,' Stavros replied to his boss. 'They will.' They both fell silent as the black limousine drove them through the Cape Town suburbs. Neither man truly believed what they had just said.

Kayley couldn't sleep. It was eleven o'clock. Before she lay in her customary bath, she turned on satellite television. She chose the news. CNN were broadcasting Archimedes' speech. Kayley watched attentively.

'We had that disease in Atlantis a hundred years ago. We have the antidote as well,' she muttered to herself. Then she wheeled herself to her bath but not before she had told David about it. David sat beside her in her bath as they talked about the killer virus in Africa.

'We have to go back to Atlantis. We can get the antidote. We must let President Ajax know we can save people's lives,' she said as she settled back to sleep. David kissed her cheek and then disappeared to his bed in his adjoining suite. They both slept well that night.

Chapter Eighteen

David and Kayley sat in Kayley's bedroom, deliberating what to do next. It was a clear autumn morning and the sun shone brightly through the windows, making patterns on the floor. The swish Tiensin Chinese rug was highlighted with rays of bright sunlight. It made a beautiful pattern on the floor. David took in the scene. Kayley was seated in her wheelchair at the desk. She looked out at the city skyline. David was drunk on her beauty. She did not have her protective blanket over her so he could see clearly her beautifully constructed fish tail. He took in the scales along the sides. She wore a prim and proper Broderie Anglaise blouse. She looked exquisite.

David was deeply in love with her but she was a mermaid. David didn't like to think of the practical problems. He was happy to be in the presence of such a beautiful creature. That was enough.

Her hair looked bright against the pale walls. It covered her breasts and also went down the back of the wheelchair. Her lips were gently pursed upwards and her eyes – Bambi-like orbs – were a gentle reddish colour today. Red was for passion in Atlantis. David wondered what thoughts caused Kayley to be full of poignant emotion. Today she was the most beautiful woman in the world. David smiled to himself, as lovers do.

'Yes, we will return to Atlantis. Our job has been done here. We've foiled the rebels' attempt to bring down weapons and we need the serum to kill the deadly virus in Africa. My people have it in Atlantis. It isn't a problem.' She seemed to be talking to herself as much as David. Finally, after a long pause, she looked at David.

'Yes, I agree,' he replied.

'I will write to President Ajax right away,' she continued.

'OK,' David agreed.

Kayley took hold of the writing implements on the desk. She

wrote studiously for several minutes. David continued to drink in her beauty as she wrote. She finished her letter. It was short and to the point:

Dear President Ajax,

We understand you are grappling with a deadly killer virus which has devastated your people in Africa in recent weeks. We can help you overcome it. We have access to an antidote but it will take a week for us to get it. We will contact you when we have it.

Yours sincerely,

Kayley Masterson and David McGuinness

'That's excellent, princess.' David smiled at the brevity and concise nature of the letter. She was perfect at everything. What a woman! But she wasn't a woman... she was half-fish, half-woman. That bothered David. Still, that was part of her charm. Had she been just a woman, he wouldn't have been so protective of her. Funny, really, these thoughts passing through David's mind. Suddenly, Kayley broke the silence.

'Right, we'll post it immediately. Now we can set about getting back to Atlantis. I have missed my home.'

'I'm beginning to understand what you mean about Atlantis. I miss it too, princess,' he replied. Then they began to talk about the return journey. Kayley's eyes were blood red. David kissed her gently, full on the lips. Her lips parted. His tongue delved into her mouth sensually. The sun shone onto them as they expressed their special kind of unique love. The things of earth ceased to be important.

'We do not know what to do,' the old man said gravely. Porthos, for all his expertise and experience, seemed genuinely at a loss. He had ruled with goodness, purity and love. He had never in his 250 years had to face evil head-on. It was all new to him. He floundered for words.

'Presiding Minister Ka has been abducted and is being held hostage by Jewel in our arena.' The arena was where the Elders and the Presiding Minister sat to pass laws and rule the tiny kingship. It was a circular structure embellished by marble. There were seats on the left and on the right. Each side was for the separate parties. Facing them was the large throne, the seat of the Presiding Elder. It was largely made of semi-precious amethyst and built centuries ago for the first Presiding Elder by Julius I, their 'ruler for good'. The place itself was compact with doors at the back and at the front. The ceiling was low and lights blazed over the room.

Ka had gone into the arena in the morning and Jewel had captured him, armed with an AK-47. He had tied him to the throne in the centre of the room.

Porthos had entered by the front door, swimming peacefully in, only to be ordered to adhere to Jewel's terms. Jewel demanded that the quorum hand over power to him otherwise he would simply kill Ka and set on the others with his forces. He did not divulge how many troops he had. Jewel was using evil to battle against good. Porthos and the Atlantean Elders were used to ruling with good and not evil. He was at a loss as to how to fight Jewel, never having come up against so much evil. The other Elders were in the same boat. It was a thousand years ago that Julius I had conquered the last evil uprising. Atlantis had had peace for the remaining thousand years. None of the Elders were adept at fighting evil. They were like children against a violent giant.

'What can we do?' Porthos seemed to mutter to himself as much as to his audience. Leila sat next to him and then Kayley and David with Spero manning the door as always. He was more of a friend than a servant. They were in their lounge and it was midday.

'We are peace-loving people,' Leila continued speaking for all of them. 'We do not know how to tackle warlike people. We have no experience of it. Atlantis has been a peace-loving state for a thousand years.' The words seemed to reverberate against the marble ceiling and return to them.

There was a long silence. No one seemed to have anything to say.

Then David spoke up. He was embarrassed at first, aware that he was human and that this was not his city, not his fight. But he seemed to sense that he was the only one with the key. By dint of his worldly experience he was able to provide an answer. He was used to wars and violence – and this was merely a simple abduction with threats.

'I am a part-time policeman on earth. We are used to fighting against violence and evil all the time up there. If you choose to become evil, you will lose your supernatural powers to heal and be telepathic. Let me deal with this Jewel character. I'm used to policing the streets of Wandsworth and Brixton in London. We have plenty of violent abductions up there. Let me handle this for you.'

There was a deathly silence. David could almost hear them taking it all in. It was not an easy decision for the old merman and his wife. David could tell that they had their pride to deal with as well as all this. He kept silent, waiting for them to reply. Finally, Porthos spoke up.

'We have an Elders' council meeting in an hour. I would like you and Kayley to come with us to it. We can discuss it there with our fellow Elders. We can come to a decision.'

'I would be delighted to,' David responded.

'Me too, daddy,' Kayley joined in.

They set about eating lunch. The hour passed quickly.

The fellow Elders began arriving. They were ushered in to the study, a long room with eight seats separated by ceramic tables. Its main colour was an emerald green. Made of marble, it had a thin red line across the centre of the walls. There were up-lighters in the four corners of the angular room. The faces of the Elders were grim. They were very child-like. They were not so much frightened of losing power as seeing violence and evil pervade the tranquil kingdom of Atlantis. They chatted softly to one another. Used to each other, they had been through many experiences together but they had always ruled through good and never by evil. It was as though they were stripped naked. They swam to their seats and awaited their host's call to order.

'Now, we are meeting here to discuss the issue of Ka's abduction,' Porthos began lamely. He was helpless in this situation. The Elders were equally helpless. They talked for some time, reaching no verdict.

'We risk losing the peaceful foundation with which we have prospered this last thousand years,' Zoltan observed.

'We have a responsibility to our young mermen and mermaids. If they become evil, they will lose their supernatural powers,' Dathan added. Although they sat on opposite sides usually, they were all united over this serious issue. It was the worst example of danger anyone in the room had ever known. Except for David...

David felt himself to be an outsider but he felt a hand guiding him as he spoke.

'Let me combat this man, friends. I'm a part-time police officer on earth and I'm used to this sort of thing. My police training will help me to fight him. I don't know if I can save Ka but I'm prepared to try,' David paused. 'If you people go against him will not you lose your supernatural powers? And those powers give you the wisdom to rule this city. I have no such problem. Let it be me. Even if I fail, we will have tried. What have you to lose?'

They seemed to take in what David suggested, then Porthos spoke, ominously. 'We could let David have the bombs, firearms and handguns that we have kept secretly locked in the crypt for a thousand years.'

Zoltan replied, 'He could get used to the weapons in our theatre.'

'The bombs, I am told, can blow open a marble door,' Dathan added.

'We shall vote on it, beloved,' Porthos mustered his people. The five mermen voted unanimously for David to have his chance to combat Jewel. The Atlantis theatre was a long pillared courtyard in Zoltan's luxurious home. It was approximately a hundred feet in length and it would be quite easy to fire a handgun at a makeshift target there. Zoltan, having shaken David's hand enthusiastically, told him about it as they took refreshments. They clustered around him like children around Father Christmas.

David prayed that he would be able to outmanoeuvre Jewel. He needed some target practice. And he needed to formulate a plan.

Porthos let David into the crypt. The bombs were like grenades, oval shaped. There was a button you pushed before you threw them. They took ten seconds to detonate. *If they're able to blow open an Atlantean marble door they're more sophisticated than earth's grenades*, David smiled to himself. This was such an innovative and wonderful people. The handguns were oval with a thin handle and a circular trigger which was more of a button. David was very pleased with his weapons. He was amazed that Atlantis had refined such munitions over a thousand years ago. There was, surprisingly, an AK-47, David noticed, taken from a desert warrior according to Porthos and left there for safety.

What a people!

He practised with the new handguns in Zoltan's theatre. It didn't take him long to adjust to the handgun. It was more mobile than guns he was used to and sent out a green sort of light beam which exploded its target on impact. David got used to its range. Although the handgun was lethal in Julius's time, Atlantis had advanced so much medically that their doctors could save the life of someone wounded by one nowadays.

He would be ready for Jewel.

He needed Kayley to make a diversion though. They agreed that Kayley, armed with the AK-47, and three other mermaids, would blast the front entrance of the Atlantis arena with bombs. David would blow open the rear entrance and hopefully be able to save Ka. He would wait for fifteen seconds after the explosions at the front. They banked on Jewel's going to investigate the bombing at the front door. If David was quick he could swim in and attack Jewel from the rear.

The four of them rehearsed the manoeuvre until they were blue in the face. They planned the attack for five in the morning. A time when Jewel would be most vulnerable. Just before morning. With a little luck, he'd be half asleep. Surprise was a weapon David had learnt to use in his police raids.

At four o'clock in the morning they met in Porthos' study. His blue house was only a stone's throw away from the Atlantis arena.

They rehearsed the manoeuvre one last time. Surprise was their secret weapon and David prayed it would catch Jewel unawares.

At five they were all in their battle positions. Kayley and her mermaids had swum to the front of the arena, and positioned themselves outside the front door. Kayley threw a bomb. Her mermaids threw two more. They waited ten seconds. The three bombs exploded at almost the same time. The explosions rang out.

There was a flurry of dust at the entrance of the huge marble door. *It must have woken Jewel,* Kayley thought. Surely he'd go to investigate the explosion at the front. That would give David time to expose the back and get to Ka.

David heard the three explosions at the back of the building. He had swum to a position thirty feet from the giant marble back door. He waited for the agreed fifteen seconds, then he threw two bombs at the back door. Ten seconds passed. Then two explosions rang out and a cacophony of dust exploded into the air. David kept his head down and pinned back his ears.

He waited.

Then he looked up.

There was a great hole in the marble door. David swam through the hole. His eyes had to accustom themselves to the darkness for there were no lights on in the auditorium. Slowly his eyes adjusted. He moved to the huge throne. He could only see the back of it from the rear door.

Suddenly he saw Jewel. He was a few feet from the great throne; swimming with an AK-47. Then Jewel reached the steps approaching the throne and he pointed the AK-47 at it. In the dark, David made out the face of Ka. As he peered he saw that Ka was tied to the throne by ropes. Jewel had pointed his AK-47 at his head.

'Put down your bombs and handgun, earthling,' Jewel snarled. He held the trump card; Ka had a gun to his head

David threw his weapons down.

'Come here, earthling,' Jewel ordered.

David obeyed. He swam next to Jewel. Surrender was the only way. *Perhaps I'll find some way to disarm Jewel later*, thought David.

'Go to the nearest chair.'

David reached the chair. Jewel began to tie David to it. Suddenly a crack rang out that broke through the silence. Jewel jerked and grimaced, then he grabbed his head and fell to the water. A hole appeared in his head. It became ruddy with blood. He was dead; the blood darkened the water. David wearily turned to where the shot had come from. Kayley and her three mermaids swam to him. A mermaid untied Ka, who was tired but unharmed.

'Thank you, my children,' said Ka.

Kayley reached out for David. They kissed. Their love was stronger than an AK-47 bullet. They smiled at each other as they hugged each other closely.

'A mermaid and a man. Some combination,' David muttered.

'The best, my love,' came her reply. Then they kissed again. This time a long, lingering kiss.

The next day at eleven the Elders and Porthos and Leila made David an honorary citizen of Atlantis at a special meeting in the well-lit arena. David felt honoured. Kayley was by his side. Ka spoke.

'We have taken all the rebels prisoner now. I not only bestow on you an honorary citizenship of Atlantis but I bestow my blessing on the love you have for Kayley, the daughter of Porthos and Leila. May fortune bless your union and may peace reign in Atlantis as long as I am her Presiding Elder. As it is written so shall it be done.'

There was a blessing on their liaison, and David reached out for Kayley and drew her to him. Again they kissed. This time in public. A slow, lingering kiss that only lovers can give.

Their love would last for ever... because love is for ever. The difference between them mattered little. What mattered was their sweet union. That day David and Kayley confirmed their love in public.

Porthos smiled at Leila. 'Our little one has found a mate, my wife,' he said.

'Indeed she has, my husband,' replied Leila, putting her hand in his. Then they kissed.

Chapter Nineteen

Kayley and David's evening was filled with much poignancy; it was potentially their last together. Their differences were nowhere on their minds. They behaved like star-struck teenagers. Kayley took David on a guided tour of Atlantis. Heaven under the sea. There were bridges over the public buildings with seating over the waterways. You were positioned at water level on a sort of escalator which put you on the glass seating with a special view of the waterways. The sanitation was more sophisticated than on earth. Each home had glass drains which went below the rocks on which the city sat. Five miles deep.

They talked. And kissed. Then they came up for breath.

Kayley told David all about his dilemma. She spoke into David's mind. David was gob-smacked. He loved Kayley very deeply. Their child-like lovemaking had so much meaning for them both. To just trace his finger over her svelte skin gave David goose-pimples. He felt so young. One of the qualities Kayley possessed was a child-like view of life. She saw life in an uncomplicated way. It was catching. David was well and truly caught!

They talked of David's big step in becoming an Atlantean. Kayley did not press David. It had to be his decision. The hours passed and they got ready to go back for what could be the last time.

'Africa needs us.' Kayley was being practical. 'Yes, my love,' David smiled at her.

Six days after they had left earth David and Kayley, armed with her trusty wheelchair and blanket, were met at Kinshasa airport by a representative of Archimedes Ajax, Lieutenant-Colonel Stavros Sealey.

'I trust your flight was good.' They had flown from New York on Ajax's Lear jet. The opulence was repugnant to Kayley who was not materialistic.

In their luggage was the serum, packaged with great protection and care. They carried enough for a nation. Africa was now in a state of panic. South Africa, Zaire and Kenya bore the main brunt of what was happening. The rest of the countries were, at the time, safe. It was a race to find a cure.

So this couple were important.

Archimedes has rolled out the red carpet. He was unable to come but Stavros Sealey was the next best thing. Ajax hadn't questioned where they'd come from. The crippled girl had talked of research in New York. It had gone through Archimedes like the illness itself; he was desperate.

South Africa had become a crazy land. The streets of the big cities had become hunting grounds. The rich Afrikaners stayed at home. There was murder, rape and pillaging in Cape Town, Johannesburg, Durban and Port Elizabeth. The law ceased to exist. Gangs of crazy blacks ransacked the shops and streets. The police had been attacked by the disease and were seriously depleted in number. They had fought for peace but they lost.

Jungle law prevailed. The army, who were hardest hit, were trying to protect the streets. Armoured cars escorted people to supermarkets and protected innocents who sought to purchase supplies.

Many supermarkets increased their prices so that only the rich could afford everyday items. Gangs of blacks victimised innocent people, seizing them and kidnapping them. Life was cheap in South Africa.

Zaire, because Ajax's special forces were evident, was just about keeping her head above water. But for how long? Ajax visited his disease-ridden troops. He knew no fear. He possessed the philosophy that if he was going to contract the disease, it was meant to be.

He declared martial law in Zaire. There was martial law in Kenya, too, but each army had continued to be depleted. They had to stop the disease. The death toll rose past the 3,000 mark.

Ajax was desperate.

In South Africa the poor blacks laid waste to the rich shopping areas. They threw stones at the shop windows. Once inside they helped themselves to the spoils. Some districts were better than others. This was all exacerbated because the army had been asked to help control other lands.

Ajax had a rebellion on his hands. The disease-ridden were kept in schools, municipal buildings and churches. People were dropping like flies.

When would it spread to Kenya and Zaire? And the rest? It was into this maelstrom that Kayley and David came.

A bullet-proof limousine sped them to Ajax's palatial residence, where a squadron of medics were waiting to be briefed by Kayley, who had yet to see the antidote have the same effect in modern-day Africa that it had had in Atlantis.

She knew that when the serum entered a man's body it took a day to turn the tide. Kayley was secretly holding her breath. She did not tell David of her doubts. It was in the lap of the gods. She was inwardly nervous. Her supernatural power of prophecy was absent. It was because she was living in her emotions – and not in her spirit. This was why she was not feeling spiritually successful.

She briefed the crowd of doctors, headed by Victor Shasa and his German, British and American colleagues. They set about injecting everyone in Kinshasa and the major towns there. The whole operation took a day. The medics were thorough.

Now all they could do was wait. The serum was sent to South Africa and Kenya. Both countries had doctors standing by. That took half a day longer.

Archimedes Ajax collapsed in his office. He just lost consciousness. His male secretary alerted Colonel Sealey.

'Make his quarters a quarantined medical unit,' Sealey ordered, 'Damn, damn, *damn!*' he said to himself.

Just then Victor Shasa phoned.

'It's working, Colonel,' Victor announced jubilantly. 'Their temperatures are going down and the fever is abating.'

'Are you sure?' Sealey needed reassurance.

'It will really be about three days before we can be sure but the signs are promising. In Kinshasa alone there have been no deaths among those we have inoculated—'

'Good. Keep me informed, Doctor,' Sealey directed. Stavros Sealey instructed the nearby medical team to inoculate General Ajax.

They injected him. No change.

Ajax remained unconscious. The fever still remained. Sealey

was concerned. Archimedes Ajax had a heart condition. He had had two heart attacks. One had been slight. The second had been more serious. His doctors had told him to ease off his duties. Ajax had ignored them. He believed himself to be invincible. The serum fought Ajax's fever. Archimedes was fighting for his life. He then regained consciousness. His face had turned purple, Stavros thought. He called Victor Shasa. Shasa treated Ajax. Sealey could only look on as the experienced doctor treated his important patient.

'The serum is fighting the virus, Colonel, but his heart is giving out. It's as if he's exerting such an effort to fight the fever on his own, that his heart is giving in.'

'Will he make it?' Stavros enquired.

'It's touch and go, Colonel,' Victor spoke honestly.

'Stay with him, doctor,' Stavros ordered Shasa.

'I will let you know of any further developments as soon as they happen, my friend,' Victor assured Colonel Sealey. Stavros stormed out of the room.

'Come on, Archimedes, Africa needs you!' He muttered to the empty office. Stavros was a good lieutenant but he was lost as a leader of men. He knew his limitations and had settled for the position he held. He was Ajax's right hand man. That was as far as he could go. He needed Archimedes. He had no confidence in his own abilities. He was, however, the power behind the throne. Archimedes had done a lot of things that Stavros had not privately approved of. What would he do if he lost his superior? Just as he was familiarising himself with these thoughts the phone rang. It was Victor Shasa.

'I'm afraid we are losing him, Colonel. The fever has left him but his heart has given up. He's a big man and his heart cannot hold out.'

'Are you sure, Doctor Shasa?' Stavros demanded.

'Regretfully, yes, Colonel,' replied Victor gently.

'I'll come right away,' Stavros said. When he reached Archimedes' room, he looked straight into his eyes. Ajax looked petrified. Stavros reached for his hand and held it softly. Neither man spoke. There was no time.

Half an hour later General Archimedes Ajax was dead.

Colonel Sealey wept. The United Black African Republic had been Archimedes Ajax's dream and it was over. It was not the dream of Lieutenant-Colonel Stavros Sealey, however. That night, Sealey made a broadcast from Ajax's desk to the continent of Africa through SABCI, one of South Africa's television channels.

'Tonight at 7.55 p.m. General Archimedes Ajax died. In fighting the virus his heart gave out on him. He died of a heart attack. After much deliberation over the matter, I am disbanding the UBAR – the United Black African Republic. Africa has had too many dictatorships in her history and this is a step too far. In my role as President I wish to bring peace to Africa. All political governments shall have their powers returned to them. In Africa, common sense will prevail. There will be no central ruling party. All countries must try and live in peace from this moment onwards. I will stand down as UBAR's head of state immediately. Long live a peaceful continent of Africa, my friends. Good night.'

Stavros finished the broadcast. He had a heavy heart but he believed he had done the right thing.

It would be a matter of weeks before all the countries returned to a semblance of normality but common sense had prevailed. Archimedes had been wrong. Stavros was right. Now that he had the power he had reversed the situation. He knew that South Africa, Kenya and Zaire would recover from their epidemics. The remaining countries would return to their previous regimes in no time. Africa would recover from General Archimedes Ajax's dictatorship. Deep down Stavros Sealey knew that Africa was a great continent. She would recover – given time. He lit one of Archimedes Ajax's Havana cigars. He picked up the phone.

'Get me my car. I'm going home,' he said to the secretary.

'What do a man and a mermaid do when they are in love and want to live together?' David asked Kayley.

'Well, I'm not going to tell you. Work it out for yourself,' she shot back.

'Do you marry in Atlantis?'

'You know we do.'

'Will you be my wife, Kayley?'

'I will, David.'

'Even though I'm a man and you're a mermaid?'

'Even though… yes, it doesn't matter.'

Kayley turned and kissed David. Their hearts sang a love song. Time stood still.